Get
REAL

The Coffee Song (They've got an awful lot of coffee in Brazil)
Written and composed by Bob Hilliard and Dick Miles © 1946
by Valiant Music Co. Inc., NY
Latin-American Music Publishing Co. Ltd., London

First published in Great Britain in hardback
by HarperCollins *Children's Books* 2005
First published in Great Britain in paperback
by HarperCollins *Children's Books* 2005
HarperCollins *Children's Books* is a division of
HarperCollins*Publishers* Ltd 77-85 Fulham Palace Road,
Hammersmith, London W6 8JB

The HarperCollins *Children's Books* website address is
www.harpercollinschildrensbooks.co.uk

1 3 5 7 9 8 6 4 2

ISBN 0 00 714281 1

Printed and bound in England by Clays Ltd, St Ives plc

Get REAL

MIMI THEBO

HarperCollins *Children's Books*

To the memory of Harry Dent

Harry Dent was my husband's grandfather. I never knew him, but I know a little of how special he was because I've heard all the stories.

One of the best is a secret Andy and his grandfather kept. Every night, after Andy had gone to bed, Harry would come and baby-sit while Andy's dad picked up Andy's mum from work. And, every night, Andy would listen for the tap of his grandfather's shoes coming down the passage. As soon as he heard Dad's car start, Andy scampered downstairs. He'd chat and watch telly on his grandad's lap until they heard the car returning. Then he'd run back to his bed. Andy didn't tell his parents the truth about those nights until he was nearly forty!

That secret, that family, and all the wonderful people I have known in the West Riding grew into Get Real. My thanks to my in-laws, Margaret and Tony Wadsworth, the hardworking teachers and students at Cathedral School (Artie didn't end up going there, but he'd have probably been happier if he did), Wakefield-Emley FC, the neighbours at Willerton Close, Ian Southwell and Adie Bashforth (wherever they may be), and all our old friends.

I also need to thank the memory of my own amazing grandparents, Julia Ellen and Daniel Patrick Ritter, and all the grandparents of my daughter Olivia – Margaret and Tony again as well as my mother, Katy Beard – for giving her the same steadfast and selfless love I tried to write about in this book.

Prologue

We were working with percentages and Mr Jankovich was talking about compound interest. I'd done all this at home. My parents are in business and their business spills over into home, as well. So sometimes when I was doing something at school, I'd realise that I already knew how to do it from helping Mum and Dad at home. I'd been working out rates of compound interest since I was about seven years old – even the twins could do compound interest.

I could see the rugby pitch from the window. I noticed that they'd have to re-mark it for Friday's match. It had been raining all week and the grass was a mess. You could hardly tell where the touch line was supposed to be.

I just thought that for a second, but that's all it took. My brain kind of slipped out of control. I thought about how much I hated rugby and how I wished our school wasn't too posh to have proper football, because then I wouldn't have to trail miles to train and all my matches would be on weekdays. Then I thought about how interesting it is to watch somebody marking a pitch and then about the big lawnmower they use at our ground, and then I kind of heard and smelled grass being cut, and then I was somewhere else.

I don't know where or when it was or if it ever actually happened. If it did, I think it was after the twins were born. Mum was bigger than she is now. Not fat exactly, but bigger. Softer. She didn't have that pinched look in her face that she gets.

It's warm and the sun is shining. There's a ball – there's always a ball – but I'm not doing anything with it. I'm just sitting on the grass by Mum's chair. She's messing with my hair. We aren't saying anything, we're just sitting there. I

lean my head back against Mum's leg and I feel
her kind of quietly moan, not a bad moan or
anything, but just a little sound that means
she's happy. There isn't anything to do. There
isn't anyone waiting or anything. We just relax.

'Mr Connor?'

But there *was* someone waiting, of course.
Mr Jankovich was waiting for me to answer. I
hadn't even had my eyes closed. I didn't even
have to blink or anything. Mum, the sun, the
grass all disappeared and I was back in maths.

I said, 'Sorry?' and Mr Jankovich sighed. He
looked tired. His face was usually pretty pink,
but that day it looked kind of grey. He had dark
marks under his eyes. He rubbed them with one
hand while he talked.

'Mr Connor, I asked you what the monthly
repayment of a loan of £12,000 over five years
would be if the annual percentage rate was
4.9%.'

I tapped into my calculator while he spoke and
so was able to say, '£249 exactly,' quite quickly.

Mr Jankovich was surprised that I'd

answered. His tired eyes opened up a bit more. But then they narrowed again.

'Yes, well,' he said, and his voice was sharp and cold. 'See me after class in any case.'

Across the room, Matt rolled his eyes. He made his mouth say, 'Not again!'

I shrugged. I wanted to look out the window again, but I didn't know where it would take me if I did. So I made a game of working out the problems quicker than Mr Jankovich could explain them.

It wasn't the last lesson of the day and we both had places to go. Mr Jankovich got straight to the point. 'Your father told me about your visualisation exercises. Is that what you were doing?'

My visualisation exercises. Every hour I was supposed to picture myself scoring a goal or crossing to another player who scores. Dad had even told my *teachers* about it so I wouldn't get into trouble doing it during school. He needn't have bothered. I never remembered to do it.

But it was a way out of trouble. All I had to

do was say 'Yes'. It wasn't true, but it was useful. That's what Dad says when he's being 'economical with the truth', as he puts it. Sometimes he'll tell a whopper on the phone and wink at me. My mum's face always looks a little more pinched when he does that.

'Don't be economical wi' t' truth,' Grandad used to say. 'Honesty is like good shoes, cheaper in t' long run.'

Mr Jankovich was waiting. I opened my mouth.

'You look tired' is what came out of it. It surprised us both.

He smiled. 'I have a new baby, remember? She hasn't learned how to sleep yet.'

People started coming in for the next lesson. Mr Jankovich said, 'Artie, you've got to stop daydreaming in class. Your Dad's right about the power of your mind, and you need to learn to control it.'

That made sense. I nodded.

He jerked his head to the door. 'Naff off,' he said.

And I did.

*

I think about that day and that conversation a lot, lately. It was kind of the beginning of something. Dad and Mr Jankovich were right, I guess. In a way, I suppose I made everything happen, only it didn't feel like power.

It was the day Grandad put the kettle in the fridge, and I didn't feel powerful at all. I felt helpless – really, really helpless.

1. Ring a Ding Ding

There's about six or seven of us around the same age on the estate, but Matt is the only one who ended up going to the grammar school with me. He's still eleven but I'm twelve, nearly a year older than him. It just worked out that way, with when my birthday is. I'm always nearly a year older than lots of people in my class.

Now, most of the other kids at our school live on the other side of town, and don't walk home our way. I guess when I started, earlier that year, I kind of enjoyed how everyone wanted to come back with me. My mates from the estate are used to us being there, you know? It's not like they don't know we have a pool and a wall-sized plasma-screen telly and all the latest games stuff and the billards table and everything, but they don't actually think about it all the time they're with me.

I mean, if it's a hot day or something and we've been, I don't know, playing tennis down by the library or something, and someone says, 'Eh, Artie, let's go round yours and swim,' we might all go to ours. If Mum or Dad are home, or if we can get Grandad to trail the twins up the street. But that's not *why* they play tennis with me. Of course, if we really *were* playing tennis, I'd have brought the big tennis bag down to the courts that Dad kept full of test rackets and balls and things. Mum and Dad are sports agents, and two or three manufacturers give him and Mum a sample of pretty much everything they make. But that's not why they'd play with me either.

With my mates from the estate, all the extras are nice, but they're not *important*. Mum and Dad founded their own agency a few years ago and have been doing really well ever since. But if they went broke tomorrow and we lost everything, my mates from the estate would still play tennis with me. We'd just stay a little hotter at the end of the day, that's all, without the pool.

But for a while I was kind of an arse and was letting the pretty girls and the guys who have really important dads come home with me after school, and kind of ignoring Matt. And then, after about a month of it, I realised I'd been kind of an arse and started going home with just Matt again.

What really did it was the look on the posh kids' faces when we got back to ours – only not ours, Grandad's. Grandad has looked after me since we came back from London. My mum was born in his house and my dad was born three streets over, but his parents are dead. Grandad's still alive and still lives where he always has lived. When Mum and Dad started making big money, they moved half the business north. And then they bought two houses just down the road, semis, and knocked them through to make ours. They added some extensions, too, kind of glass boxes. It's really nice, actually, and got in all kinds of magazines. It even won an award.

So when I brought the posh kids back and we walked right past our really nice house and down the little street to the estate and Grandad's semi, their faces would fall. Some of them weren't even particularly nice to Grandad and kind of sneered at his orange kitchen and his plastic cups, and even his Jammie Dodgers.

Matt wasn't like that.

He smiled when we rang the bell and Grandad threw open the door.

I suppose it wasn't all the posh kids' fault. Grandad is a little hard to take if you aren't used to him.

And that day, he was a little harder to take than usual.

I saw it straight away, though I couldn't say exactly why. His cardigan looked a little more tatty, his wild white hair looked a little more wiry. He was singing, as usual, something about his heart going, 'ring a ding ding, ring a ding ding, ring a ding ding.' The bell must have set him off.

Usually, when I first see Grandad, or when we're at the supermarket or something and I turn back and look at him, I think, *Grandad might look a bit odd, if you didn't know him*. But that day I thought, *Grandad might look like a complete loon if you didn't know him.*

It had been happening for a while. Once he nearly put shoe polish on the twins' sandwiches. And I was used to his cardigan being buttoned up wrong, the milk being in the cupboard, him forgetting to take his money to the supermarket. Dad had already taken his car keys away. But this was something different, something *else*.

'Come in!' he said, when he'd stopped singing, even though we were already in. 'Come in, come in, come in, come in, come in.'

I looked through into the living room. The twins were watching telly. I went and switched it off. 'Homework,' I said.

'Oh, Artie, just one more...'

But I was stern. 'I'll bring you a cup of tea through,' I said and pointed to the table. Neil put his tongue out at me, but Glynnis didn't seem to mind. I don't think Neil really minded, either. They knew they weren't supposed to be allowed telly on a school afternoon. Trying it on felt normal; getting away with it felt weird. They actually looked happier once they were grumbling at the table.

Back in the kitchen, Matt looked strange now, too. He was smiling and nodding at Grandad, but you could tell there was something wrong. I took a sip of my tea and then remembered I'd promised the twins a cuppa, and I might as well make it while the kettle was still hot. But when I looked for the kettle, it wasn't there.

The little ring it sat on was there and the lead was there, but the kettle wasn't. It wasn't on the work surface. I went to the cupboard where Grandad sometimes stows the milk by mistake. The milk was there, but the kettle wasn't. Grandad was talking to Matt about the time he won best dahlia at the flower show. It was before I was born, but he was as excited talking about it as if it was yesterday.

Matt was still smiling and nodding but he kind of pointed with his eyes to the refrigerator. When I opened the fridge door, a big gust of steam came out. Grandad had put the kettle on the top shelf of the fridge! I pulled it out and put it on the work surface. Grandad must have seen me, but he didn't stop talking for a second. The fridge was a mess. Everything was really wet. I got the dishcloth and did the best I could, but then I noticed the margarine tub had melted on one side and so had the spread inside it. It was starting to leak out on to the shelf. I kind of wrapped it in the dishcloth to get it to the bin.

Grandad was still talking.

So then I put the dishcloth in the washer, got some kitchen roll and tried to get the marge off the top shelf, but it spread everywhere.

Grandad was *still* talking.

At first I didn't think he'd even noticed. But while I was getting more kitchen roll, I saw his face and he was just talking – talking desperately. Sweat was on his forehead and he looked like he was about to cry. Matt was frozen by the door. I kind of prised the mug out of Matt's hand, told him I'd see him tomorrow and shoved him out the door. Then I pushed Grandad down on to the stool.

I made the twins a quick cup of tea so they'd stay out of the kitchen and took it through with a plateful of biscuits.

Grandad was still talking when I went into the lounge, but he'd shut up by the time I came back.

We looked at each other for a moment, and then he said, very reasonably and normally, 'There's some of those cleaning wipes under t' sink. They'll get t' marge up.'

And I said, 'Yeah. OK,' and got them and they did.

And then we looked at each other again. He said, 'I'm sorry, Tony.'

Tony is my Dad's name. Whenever Grandad is upset, he does that.

I said, 'It's OK. But you have to be careful.'

He nodded, and brushed his eyes with the back of his hand. I handed him my cup of tea and he took a long sip.

Just then, Mum came in, blew in, like one of those tornadoes they have in America. 'Just do it, Tina,' she said. 'Just send it. They'll understand.' She was talking into her headset. She put her bag on the work surface and covered up the microphone with her hand.

'Have you made tea yet, Dad?' she asked.

He shook his head, no. I could see he didn't trust himself to speak.

She uncovered the microphone. 'Yes, I will. Put that in the diary, will you, and update my Outlook, you know the code.' She listened for a second. 'No, tell him to talk to Trevor. *No*, tell him Trevor knows it better than I do. Yes, I know what he always says, but I'm *not* trailing down to London every time he gets the collywobbles, Tina, it's too expensive. Tell him I gave Trevor the file and Trevor knows it all better than me. Get Trev to take him to David Seaman's new restaurant. Victoria Beckham's over and eating lunch there with her mum on Thursday and she'll come say hi to Trevor, he used to do the Spice Girls, that'll impress him...' Another quick pause. 'Tina, Tina! That can wait. I've got to go. I've got to go *now*.' She clicked off the call and then, very quickly, clicked off her phone as well.

She rubbed her eyes for a second, took my cup of tea from Grandad and drank some of it before she gave it back to him. She kissed his cheek and then shouted, 'Who wants to have tea at Pizza Hut?'

The twins exploded into the kitchen. 'Me! Me!'

'Bags,' she said, and then looked at me. 'Is that yours?'

Mine was still unopened on the side. 'Yeah,' I said, 'but I can do my prep later.'

'OK, let's go!'

And we all piled into the people carrier. I saw Grandad's face at the window as he waved us off. I wanted to run back and do something – cuddle him, make him a cup of tea of his own. I knew he wouldn't dare to try another that night.

It was getting darker earlier. His face was just a white spot at the black window, shaped like all the other windows down his street. If you didn't know the street really well, it could have been anyone. And then it was gone.

2. Unforgettable

'Did you tell your mum?'

It was the first thing Matt asked and I hadn't even *considered* doing it.

'No,' I said, like Matt was insane for even asking me.

Looking back, I should have done. I should have told Mum or Dad straightaway, even before this. I should have told them about the shoe polish. I should have told them about the milk. But they were so busy right then. They'd just taken over another agency and they had a huge new client list and all the new clients wanted to meet them personally. I didn't even *see* Dad during the week, and for Mum to actually make it home in time to take us to Pizza Hut was a bit heroic of her. I got up at six like I usually do, to run and do some weight training, and she'd already left for the office in London. Dad was locked in the study. I didn't see him, but I could hear him answering emails. He was there until we left for school, if you see what I mean, in case the house caught on fire or someone got sick or something. But it wasn't like he was around.

I got the twins up and walked them to school, just like I do every morning. And then I did English, which I'm pretty good at, and Italian, which I'm not at all, and then it was time for history, and Matt and I had a chance to talk while we made a model of Pevensey Castle (we were doing the Norman invasion). So when he asked me what he asked me it was like, *Yeah, right, dump that on to Mum, of course I will.* And also like, *And just when exactly am I supposed to work that into the conversation – oh, by the way, Mum, you can't trust your own father any more.*

So I said, 'No,' in this really kind of scornful, aren't-you-stupid-for-asking way.

And it got right up Matt's nose and he said, 'Pardon me for asking.'

And then we were completely silent for a few seconds. The castle was a bit of a pain, to be honest. We had these papier-mâché stones and this kind of pulp for mortar, and the walls were OK, but trying to get the ceilings in was murder. And you had to be careful not to leave any kind of foot or hand hold on the outside because we had to make it completely impregnable. We'd been doing it for ages, and some of the other kids were doing the kind of boat the Normans had, and somebody else was doing a Norman farm, and somebody else was doing an abbey and the gardens, and two girls and this guy who was always getting told off for wearing black eyeliner were making Norman clothes for some dolls. We had to do a presentation about it soon.

Matt sighed, and I sighed too. We looked at each other. Matt said, 'What do you reckon he'll be like this afternoon?'

I said, 'Sometimes he's fine.'

And Matt said, 'I think he's getting worse, Artie. I mean, you know, I hadn't seen him in a while...'

And we both knew why. I bent my head down behind the bailey so that Matt couldn't see my face go red. Matt kept talking. '...and I really noticed it. Haven't your parents said owt?'

My parents had hardly exchanged two words with Grandad since school started. I said, 'No,' again, but this time nicely.

Matt shook his head. His face kind of closed. He didn't want to push it. Before I'd been an arse, he would have pushed it. He's a bit bossy, is Matt, but none of us really mind because he's kind with it. But he didn't push it now, and it was because I'd been an arse and he didn't trust me like he used to. That whole thing was between us, just as impregnable as the wall of the castle, and we couldn't really talk any more.

My last lesson was Biology and during it my phone went. My phone never goes, and luckily I keep it on Silent anyway because my dad says it's good policy. He says you can keep your phone on Silent and if it vibrates, you can just excuse yourself to the loo and see if whoever is calling is more important than whoever it is you're with. I didn't have to excuse myself to the loo, I just slid it out under the cover of the desk. It was Neil. Something was wrong with the twins.

I got my stuff together and when Mr Hanson asked me what I thought I was doing, I said I had a doctor's appointment and had to go. He asked where the slip was and I said, 'I don't know. I handed it in weeks ago.' And he kind of sighed and nodded, and I escaped.

I don't like to lie, but I am very good at it.

I didn't use my phone until I was out the gate. 'What is it?' I asked. I could hear Glynnis in the background whimpering like she does when something's gone really wrong, and Neil's voice was kind of high and wavery.

He said, 'Grandad's not here and there's these big kids—'

I didn't let him get any further. I said, 'I'll be there in ten minutes. Those kids start giving you ANY grief, get back into school. OK?'

And I started to run.

What with one thing and another, I do quite a lot of running and although I don't have what it takes to make a career in athletics, I'm pretty fast. But what really helped that particular run was my footy training, because it helped me dodge. During the school run our town has to be one of the busiest places on earth. I dodged between prams and jumped over bins. At one point, I even vaulted over the bonnet of a car.

I was careful, though. I'm always careful. I'm always thinking of what would happen if I suddenly wasn't there. Everyone depends on me. And there was no way I was going to do something stupid and get knocked down or break my leg or something, and leave Neil and Glynnis waiting.

But even though I was careful, I know what my body can do, and it can do quite a lot, even in school shoes and with my bag on my back. It's a twenty-minute walk from my school to the twins' school, all uphill. I was there in nine minutes.

Glynnis's little face lit up like a garden lantern when she saw me. Neil's kind of collapsed. He'd been being brave for her and now that I was there, he couldn't do it any more. He kind of snuffled when I hugged them.

Two idiots on trick bikes were on the grass verge by the road. Glynnis said, 'They've been asking me questions.' That's all she said, but I didn't like the sound of it. I gave my bag to Neil and asked him to hold it, which seemed to make him brave again.

Then I went over.

You've probably already figured out I'm a bit big. I'm naturally tall and I do quite a lot of training so I've bulked up a bit more than most kids my age. I'm not quite thirteen yet but I could easily get served in a pub. I'm always having to show my ID to get the child fare on trains and buses.

The smarter of the two idiots threw his cigarette away and jumped on to his pedals, but I'd already grabbed their handlebars. I gave his a bit of a shake and he put his feet back on the ground.

I said, 'I understand you've been asking my little sister questions. Just what is it you want to know?'

The stupider idiot laughed. It's only because I've had to learn how to control my anger on the pitch that I didn't shove his crooked teeth down his spotty little throat.

The smarter idiot said, 'We was just trying to help them. See if they needed owt, like.'

The stupider idiot giggled at this.

I said, 'I don't think they need anything you can give them.'

And then I gave them what my dad calls 'the look'. I'd practised it in the mirror and I do it sometimes in a match when I'm being marked. It *is* a bit unnerving, if you're not used to it. I'm quite dark – my hair and my eyebrows – and when I kind of go blank and do my eyes just right, I can look frightening.

I must have done it right, because their attitudes changed.

'We meant nowt by it.'

'We was just kiddin'.'

I let go of their handlebars and stepped back, saying, 'Leave them alone, all right?'

They took off like rockets.

Neil said, 'That was brilliant, Artie! That was really good!', and Glynnis smiled up at me, really shyly, like she'd just met me or something, very girly all of a sudden.

I said, 'Does that mean you're going to do your homework tonight without whinging?' And they both kind of got normal again.

When we got to Grandad's house, I rang the bell and it seemed to take for ever for him to answer the door. 'Where have you two been?' he said. 'I've looked all over the shop.' He had dust on his cardigan. He saw me looking at it and said, 'I was up in t' loft, thinking they might be up there.' He took off his cardigan and shook it out into the garden.

'Well, what's all this standing about in aid of? Come in. Tea's almost ready.'

I only had to motion with my head and Neil

and Glynnis took their places at the table and opened up their bags to get their work out.

Back in the kitchen, Grandad was turning fish fingers over on the grill tray. One side was already done. The chip-fryer light was on and he had some kitchen towel ready to drain them on. Peas jumped in a pan of boiling water and the colander was in the sink. There was squash all made in a jug, and plates and knives and forks and tumblers on a tray. He looked really pleased with himself to have done all that, to have got all that together.

I said, 'Grandad, you forgot something today.'

And his face just... it just kind of went yellow and quivered. And I couldn't do it. I couldn't tell him. I should have, but I couldn't. And what was worse was, I thought he already knew, somewhere in his mind he knew he'd forgotten to pick up the twins and he just couldn't deal with it. He'd break up entirely if he had to admit that, so his mind kind of pretended not to know.

So I said, 'Where's the tartare sauce, Grandad? You know I can't eat fish fingers without tartare sauce.'

And he was so, so happy, showing me how he'd put the sauces out on the table already, that my eyes got wet, like they wanted to cry. He said, 'It's under control, Artie. Sit yoursen down and start on that homework. I'll bring it through.'

I went into the lounge and sat down at the table. Neil and Glynnis looked a question at me and I shook my head. I said, 'I couldn't tell him.'

And Glynnis said, 'I know. We heard.'

And Neil said, 'What are we going to do? What if he forgets again?'

The good thing about twins is that there's two of them. I would never have suggested what I suggested if there was just one of them, but two of them could do it because they'd be together. I said, 'Do you think you could walk to my school every day? If I showed you the way? There's only two crossings.'

We could hear Grandad singing in the kitchen. 'Unforgettable, la la la la...'

Neil sighed. 'I think we'd better,' he said.

3. Let's Get Away From it All

It was Friday. I'd kind of forgotten, what with everything else, that it was Friday. We'd barely swallowed our tea before Dad was there, telling us to get our stuff together and clear out down to ours. Dad's not like Mum. Even when he's tired or busy, he still has a sharp eye. It was working now, darting around the kitchen and the living room, kind of checking that everything was still OK. I could see Grandad was trying really hard not to look around and check himself, which would give the whole thing away. The twins and I were packed up in no time.

Dad said, 'Do you want a hand with the washing-up before we leave?'

And Grandad said, 'Don't be daft.'

He was at the sink when we walked out, singing about bluebirds and the white cliffs of Dover. He didn't look at all sad. He just looked relieved.

When we got home, the people carrier was all washed and the back was stuffed full of gear. Dad ran up to shower and change, and the twins knew enough to do the same without being told. They were used to the kind of weekends we had now.

This was going to be another complicated one, made a little easier by the fact that my side was playing at home this week, so the match was on Saturday. We have two grounds – the Colliery Ground, by the mine where the club started, and Bon Place, the league ground we share with the local rugby club. Everyone else in our league has to play on Sunday because they only have one ground, but our home matches are on Saturday.

So Mum and I were going to meet Dad and the twins tomorrow, after the match, and I didn't have to run around and shower or anything. Instead, I kind of wandered around downstairs for a little while.

These days we spent hardly any time at home. It's a fantastic house, but we might as well have just had three *en-suite* bedrooms and a toaster, for all the use we made of it. There was the enormous telly, with the big cream leather sofas, each on their own island of fluffy sheepskin. There was the games station with its own screen. There was the library area, where the sound system also lived. It had a bank of switches behind a cherry-wood panel the twins weren't allowed to touch. If we were having trouble waking up on one of Dad's mornings, he'd just blast us out of bed using the integrated speaker system and some of his old heavy-metal music. You'd just be lying there, thinking 'five more minutes' and suddenly Metallica or something would make everything in the room rattle, including your teeth.

The big glass doors looked out over the back, which was planted so cleverly we had enough privacy for my mum to sunbathe without her top on, if she wanted. If she was actually home on a sunny day and actually had five minutes to sit in the garden, on one of the really nice loungers that looked uncomfortable but weren't. She never did, though.

I went into the kitchen and opened the fridge. It was always surprising to see the food Daily Dozen left there. Daily Dozen did the cleaning and the laundry and the shopping, and stuff like that. Mum gave them lists. I saw one of them once, her name was Marcia. I saw another one a week later and it was somebody else.

I couldn't remember the last time we ate at the big pine table. For a minute, I played this game trying to remember what our plates and our forks and stuff looked like. I couldn't, until I opened up a drawer, and then it kind of bothered me when I saw the pattern on the silverware, the scroll bit, the little rose on the top. And I closed the drawer again.

My Mum came in from the study. She was yawning and she still had her work clothes on. She asked, 'Are you hungry, Artie?'

Just then Dad and the twins came clattering down the stairs. Mum turned to Dad, and her whole attention was on him. She was kind of looking him over and patting him down and reminding him where he was going and how to get there and asking if he had this and that and telling him what was packed in the people carrier and which bag was who's.

He told the twins to get into the car and they gave Mum a cuddle and went.

Then he reminded her of where they were going to meet tomorrow afternoon and what time and how to reach him if there was a problem, because there are no phone masts at sea. I was just standing there and watching. I think they forgot about me, because just for a moment, they kind of collapsed into each other. Dad's arms were full of gear and Mum still had a folder in one hand and a pen in the other, so they didn't even hold each other. They just leaned and it seemed like they were *smelling* each other, more than anything else. And then Dad was gone, shouting at the twins to sit down and buckle up and choose a DVD to watch *without* fighting. And Mum put her folder down on the kitchen work surface and her pen on top of it, and looked at me.

She said, 'Now, Artie. After your match, we'll get the train to King's Cross and then there's a car that's going to pick us up and take us to Dover. So we'll all meet up on board in time for tea.'

Great. I'd be absolutely shattered.

'Jonty's oldest boy isn't going to be able to make it...'

Pity. I liked him.

'But the one your age is sailing with us...'

Pity. I didn't like him.

'And the Owen girl is coming along.'

Hmm. Things were looking up.

'We're all going to get a sailor's start on Monday and just come up from London in time for school. Can you take the twins from King's Cross?'

I nodded. She rubbed her eyes. I said, 'Why don't you take out your contacts and wear your glasses?'

She said, 'I'm taking you out to see a film.'

'Why don't we just watch one here?' I pointed to the big cabinet. It was stuffed full of videos and DVDs. And we had TiVo, too, and never got round to watching all the things it recorded for us.

And she said, 'Well... the new Leeds striker? He has a little brother...'

I didn't say anything else. I just nodded and went upstairs to shower.

My clothes were all laid out. I mean ALL laid out.

There were really nice jeans and a dead trendy top laid out on the bed, with silky socks, black knit boxers and some Italian loafers. On the chair was an outfit a lot like it and a bag with my footy kit. I opened the footy kit bag and my sailing stuff was under my kit. There was a special bag for my boots inside and another special bag for the kit itself, so my other clothes didn't get dirty on the way to King's Cross, Dover and back to here.

Mum had done it all. Some time today, she'd been up here, finding just the right bag and choosing the perfect socks for me.

Something about it made me feel tired.

I really didn't want to go and watch a film with the new striker's brother. But, even more, I didn't want to let Mum down. So I showered and got into the outfit and was back down in about five minutes.

On telly, there's always all that stuff about how long women take to get ready. But my mum was already down and looked fantastic, as usual, in a very 'I'm not trying hard I'm just taking some kids to the cinema' kind of way. We got into the Audi.

Mum said, 'I'm sorry about not staying home. But right now we just have to see as many people as we can. And that means...'

And that meant parties and sailing parties and going-to-see-cricket-or-rugby-or-something parties and climbing parties and working-farm parties, and going to the cinema with someone you'd never even met. I cut her off by just saying, 'Yeah, I know.'

She said, 'If it's any help, I'm sick of it, too.'

But it wasn't any help. She and Dad were in

charge of it all. If *they* were sick of it and *they* couldn't change it, then nobody could.

We picked up the new striker's brother and somebody else who had a cousin who Leeds had just signed. They liked the car and were playing video games in the back on the twins' console. I looked out the window at the lights and the cars passing by. There was a red car that reminded me of a red toy car I had when I was tiny.

I don't know what it was about the red toy car, but I heard Mum and Dad laughing in my mind. They're laughing and they're just kind of chatting quietly and laughing some more. The sun is shining and my eyes must be closed because I can't see anything. I hear footsteps flitting by and the sound Neil makes when he runs, and then I hear Mum laugh again and Dad start up too, slow, with something really naughty in his deep chuckle. I don't even want to open my eyes and see where we are, I'm just so happy.

And then my mum says my name and I'm in front of the multiplex, under cover from the dark, pounding rain. A big plastic chicken is staring through the window at me and hundreds of people are milling about.

'Artie, you go pick up the tickets, here's my card. And here's some money for treats, but don't let them buy enough to be sick. I'll just park the car and I'll be right in.'

I did all that. By the time I sat down in my seat, it seemed like I hadn't sat down all day, like I'd been running ever since I ran to get the twins. I said, 'Ahhhh.' I didn't mean to. Mum said it too, and we looked at each other, in the light of the Pearl and Dean adverts.

And then we were busy handing the treats around and then the film started.

4. They've Got an Awful Lot of Coffee in Brazil

We won the match and I scored the winning goal and provided two others.

I should have been over the moon. But the first half, I just wasn't on the pitch. I was kind of somewhere else. I kept seeing the ball and I even had touches, but it was like someone else was running my body. I didn't have any daydreams, but I had that far-away feeling I get before I have them.

The manager had a word at half time. His word was delivered about six inches from my face and his breath was so hot it made my eyes water. It kind of snapped me out of it. I was back.

When I'm on form, something happens to me. I stop dreaming, I stop even thinking. My body moves without me. I don't have to *decide* anything. I just know where I'm going to go and what I'm going to do when I get there.

I can't even remember, a lot of the time, what actually happened in the match. I remember odd things, like if the pitch was a bit lumpy under my boots, or the size of a mole on a defender's neck. Sometimes people ask me how the game was, and I have to stop myself from mentioning things like that and actually think about things like points, which never seem all that important when I'm in *the zone*. Dad says a lot of players are that way, which is why so many of them seem a bit dazed and confused during after-match interviews, or end up talking a load of rubbish. The agency has a consultant who comes in just to teach them how to talk a bit of sense.

So, a bit of sense: we were two–nil down at half time; then I woke up and we won three–two.

I don't want to bore you with a lot of football

talk, but the three goals are important, so I have to mention them. First of all, you should know Matt plays on my team, along with a couple of other lads from my school. Matt plays forward and I'm midfield, down the left wing usually because I favour my left foot. Dad always says I'm the hope of the English side, because not many players here do.

My two assists were both to Matt – classic moves. The ball worked down the pitch to me and I crossed it to Matt's feet. My goal was something else. I'd seen Pelé do it on an old video my dad has of great goals. He's made me watch them all about a hundred times, so when the ball came in, it came to me just like it had come to Pelé and I kind of did it automatically. I was over towards the middle and it hit me in the chest. I sort of whipped around with the ball on my chest, using my chest and shoulders as it fell, while bringing my right foot (for a change) back ready to shoot. I wasn't offside, but their defence hadn't got in front of me yet, which wasn't really their fault since you'd expect me to chest it down and then to turn it, and then, if I still had a shot, to strike. But it had landed just right – really softly with no bounce – and so I was able to do it the other way. No one expected it and the keeper wasn't ready. I blasted it past him at about a million miles an hour.

The crowd went mad. Everyone was on their feet, screaming and smiling at the same time. I didn't notice it then, of course. Whenever I score a goal, it takes me funny. I have to run as fast as I can away from the goal. I only usually stop when I get to the touch line in whatever direction I've started running, or when somebody jumps on me.

No, I noticed the crowd reaction later. You see, Dad doesn't like to miss my games. He used to hire a cameraman to come and video them when he was away, until I said that was not on – *really not on at all.* So now Mum does it, like about a hundred other parents, with an ordinary hand-held one. *That's* OK, and of course Mum's got really good at it, like she does at everything.

*

So when I saw the crowd reaction, I was on board a yacht, anchored a few miles out, watching it on telly with... I don't think I should tell you any more who I'm with. Someone read what I'd written so far and said it sounded kind of like I was name dropping, and they also said I might get sued. So I've taken out all the names and won't say any more. There were a few people there, it was a big boat. And it belonged to someone my dad worked for before he became a sports agent. Dad calls him The Old Man.

Now, none of the people there wanted to give up a day's sailing. But none of them wanted to miss the highlights of the Premiership, either. And none of them had to exactly wait for *Match of the Day* to come on; they have excellent media contacts. The same little boat that brought us out from Dover at six o'clock brought out some video tapes.

All the men immediately went into the TV lounge. The ladies weren't surprised at all. The Old Man's latest wife had a little buffet set up in there with things to eat and drink. I went with them.

The first game they put on was mine. I just wanted to *die*. Dad said into my ear, 'Most lads would *kill* for a performance analysis by these minds, and you're getting it for free!' Maybe he was right. But even though there were barbecued chicken wings and pizza, I just couldn't eat. I wanted to be sick.

There was this low sofa right at the front and then behind was like a horseshoe-shaped row of really comfortable leather chairs. The Old Man and the others all sat on the chairs and I was down on the sofa with my dad, so at least I didn't have to see anyone's face.

The first half was dreadful. The Old Man kept just whizzing through the tape. I could feel my dad wasn't happy. And then I saw something, it was obvious, even on fast-forward. Twice at least, maybe three times, I'd had the ball and Matt had been right in front of an open goal and *I'd passed it to somebody else*. I hadn't even looked at him. It was like I was ignoring him, or something. Once Matt was waving really hard at me and shouting, I guess (there was no sound and luckily most people were talking about something else while they watched), but I just turned my head away like I was... I don't know. Like I was doing it on purpose. And Matt's face, on the tape, it just... he looked like he was going to cry or something.

Then the second half. The Old Man stopped fast-forwarding about two seconds in. One of the other people said, 'Ha! Looks like someone's alarm went off.' It was nothing, a simple little pass to Zack on the right, but it got everyone's attention. I don't know why.

They started to mutter at the second assist and The Old Man called my dad's name and he left me alone on the sofa. I tried really hard to hear what they were saying, but only caught a couple of words. 'Pace' was one of them, said like a question. And something about 'awareness', which I couldn't really understand at all. And then my goal came on and everyone went quiet. Mum had moved the camera to get all the crowd in, even some of the parents of the other school were smiling and shouting. My grandad was going nuts. The Old Man played it again. Grandad went nuts again. And again, and again, and again. The talking behind me got quieter.

After the match, Grandad had been so excited he could hardly talk. He called me Tony twice. And he was trying to say something about Pelé, that he recognised the trick, but he couldn't seem to remember Pelé's name. I was showered and changed and everything by then, and standing by the car while Mum talked for a moment to Matt's mum. Matt wasn't anywhere about.

Grandad's face got that desperate look again. I think I'd made it worse by looking around, not paying attention. 'You know, it's... you know,' he was saying. He scrabbled his hand through his hair and made it stick up. Zack and another kid smiled at me behind his back and I smiled back, and then felt terrible about it. But by now, Grandad's hair was sticking almost straight up in the air. It looked like Einstein or something. You *had* to smile.

And then Grandad started to sing. At least he did it quietly, but it wasn't quiet enough for Zack not to hear. And Dennis. Dennis Moore. That was the name of the other kid from my school. They heard Grandad sing, 'You can't have cherry soda, 'cause they've got to fill that quota, and the way things look I'll bet they never will.' He looked happier when he sang, 'They've got an awful lot of coffee in Brazil.'

'Pelé,' I said, both to put him out of his misery and to shut him up.

'Aye! Pelé did that!' Grandad nearly shouted it. I just kind of nodded. I was glad when Mum said we had to go.

I fell asleep on the sofa. I woke up just as they were changing tapes for the Leeds match. My dad asked me if I wanted to go down to the cabin I was sharing with Neil and Jonty's youngest boy, but I said no, I wanted to see the match. Everyone laughed. One of the other men said, 'Just as it should be.' So they left me. And I watched about two seconds and fell asleep again.

The next time I woke up, it was quieter and darker. There was just a pool of light on a table made of dark wood. There were three glasses on it and three chairs pulled around it. A cigar smouldered in a big glass ashtray, the smoke going straight up. You couldn't see the three men's faces. But I could tell one of them was The Old Man and one was my dad.

Dad was talking. He said, 'You told me two years ago the party needed my brass more than it needs me.'

The man I didn't know leaned forward a little and took the cigar, and his face came into the circle of light. And then I did know him, anyone would know him who has ever even seen a British newspaper. He's in politics. That's all I'll say. All *he* said is, 'Things have changed, Tony.'

Dad sighed and rubbed his eyes. He said, 'Local politics? If I ever got involved, I thought it would be at the national level.'

And the man said, 'From small acorns big oaks grow.' It got even quieter for a moment. I could hear the slap of the waves on the yacht's side, so far below us. I held my breath.

The Old Man said, 'You can't reach for something new with your hands full of something old.'

I breathed out as quietly as I could, thinking all the while that my dad usually does whatever The Old Man thinks is best. When he spoke, I thought he'd be saying yes. But he didn't. He said, 'I'm going to have to think about this.'

And the third man said, 'Take a while. Take till Christmas. We want you to be sure, Tony.'

Dad said, 'I'm just finding it hard to believe you want me at all. I'm more Old Labour than New Labour. You sure you've got the right man?'

The third man nodded towards the video screen. 'It's not much different from talent scouting, Tony. We needed to watch your form over a long run. We're sure.'

'Artie?' My Dad suddenly spoke a lot louder. 'Artie?' he said. 'I hope he doesn't think I can carry him to bed like I used to.'

The other two men laughed. I slunk down and

then sat up again, rubbing my eyes like I'd just woken up. My dad came over, put his arm around me and kind of pushed me out the door and down a stairwell. At the cabin door we looked at each other.

'How much did you hear?' he asked me.

His face was tight and looked yellow where it wasn't sunburned. His eyes looked bigger than usual. I'd never really seen him like that. He looked a little like Grandad does when he's having trouble, a little out of control and bothered by it.

I said, 'I heard most of it, I think. Enough anyway.'

He sighed and rubbed his eyes again. He said, 'It's what I've always wanted. But just now, it's so...' He looked at me and said, 'I'm going to have to talk to your mum about this, and I want to pick and choose the time.'

I said, 'I won't say anything.'

And he said, 'Thanks, Artie.' I started to go in the door. 'You got that Pelé move from the video, didn't you?' he asked.

I nodded. He smiled and said, 'They're already talking about picking you for the Under Fourteens. You'll be picked for the Under Nineteens in a year or so and those are well attended games, Artie. You keep scoring goals like that and you'll be able to pick your club.'

I nodded again. I knew that was what he wanted me to do, but I didn't know I was actually good enough for him to think it was possible. For a moment, my heart kind of skipped a couple of beats and I got a big lump in my throat. A professional footballer. Really.

My mind kind of raced away for a second. I saw myself on the pitch in a big stadium. That Dambusters song was playing. I looked down and I was in a white kit. I had a black armband. I was captaining England. I could smell fireworks. I had my hand on the mascot's head and I could feel her silky baby hair.

It was hard to force myself back to the boat, but it wasn't like I got much time with Dad. I wasn't going to waste it daydreaming.

He said, 'I need to start coaching you again.

This is a crucial time in your development. Somewhere, I've got to find the time.' The lump in my throat dissolved like a sweet and flooded my throat and my chest with heat. But then he said, 'Or maybe we should find someone to take you a couple of nights after school, someone from the Leeds organisation, perhaps. I could ring that guy from England Under Eighteens about it, get a name.'

And the heat slowly cooled, leaving me more tired than I've ever been in my life. I don't know if I even said good night.

5. A Foggy Day

I woke up late. It was only eight o'clock, but everyone else had been up for hours. There was a shower down the hall with stuff in it, some really nice shower gel, too. And a weird toilet next door. The less said about that the better. Then I was ready to go up on deck.

I hadn't missed anything. There was a heavy morning mist and we couldn't go anywhere. It was meant to burn off before lunch time, and we were supposed to get a little wind, as well. So we'd sail in the afternoon. We just wouldn't get as far as The Old Man had hoped.

People occupied themselves in different ways.

Three nutters, including my dad, put on wet suits and went swimming. Most of the other men played cards. My mum was talking with some of the other ladies. There were two babies on board and that kept *them* interested. I wandered around, after I'd found some breakfast. One of my grandad's stupid songs was playing in my head, about a miserable foggy day in London. I guess I was pretty low and down. But I didn't really know it yet.

The Owen girl had changed. She was great last year, really funny and smiley and lively. She had this mad curly hair and big brown eyes. But now she straightened her hair or something, because it was all flat and had highlights in it. And she was moaning about the mist and what it would do to it – like anyone cared. I tried to make a joke about it and she glared at me. Her big brown eyes were a weird colour of blue... She was using contact lenses to change the colour.

Why do girls do that? Why do they try and change everything about themselves? It doesn't really make them look better. It just makes them grumpy and horrible to be with. Girls with curly hair straighten it and girls with dark hair try and bleach it and girls with pale skin get tans and girls with freckles wear a lot of make-up trying to cover them up – and I really just don't get it. It seems such a waste of time and money, and it makes... I mean some girls look really nice in a certain way – blonde and with straight hair and blue eyes and tanned skin. But that doesn't mean *every* girl should look that way. There's lots of ways to look nice, but practically every girl I know is trying to look nice in exactly the same way.

I couldn't ask Glynnis about it; she was too young. I found her sitting near the bow on a coil of rigging, reading. You nearly always find Glynnis reading. I sat down with her for a minute. We didn't say anything.

Glynnis has very curly red hair that Mum says is like Grandad's was before he went white. She's grown it long and ties it back out of her face most of the time. I hope she never messes with it. I don't think Mum would let her.

It was so calm that even the surf against the boat was slow and quiet. You could hear Dad and the other men splashing around, working on getting hypothermia and trying to prove how hardy and 'northern' they were.

I closed my eyes and I was back in that sunny place, listening to Mum and Dad laugh together and Neil puff by, running. He's a great little lad but he'll never make an athlete. And Glynnis isn't interested. So it's just me to carry on the family tradition.

Dad played in the third division before his injury and Mum was a hurdler. She went to the Olympics twice but never got a medal. I've got her speed and Dad's coordination. Glynnis has them too, but like I said, she's not interested. At school, they'll race and she'll beat everyone, but she won't train. She goes to dance classes but she's not fanatical about it. She only seems to be fanatical about her books.

I open my eyes again and she's still reading.

I suddenly wanted to talk to her about last night, about everything Dad said: me playing for the Under Nineteens; me going pro; Dad going into politics. But I couldn't. Not just because Dad told me not to tell Mum – Glynnis could keep a secret. But because it's not fair. She shouldn't have to worry about any of that. She should just keep on being a kid. A kind of odd kid, maybe (Glynnis never has as many friends as me and Neil), but just a kid.

Dad had always said that someday he was going to turn his energies into politics. He always said that as soon as he'd made his first few million... well, surely he'd done that by now, hadn't he? If he sold the business... Why wouldn't he do it, then? He was mad for politics. Look at our names: I'm named after Arthur Scargill, who was some kind of miner who stood up to Margaret Thatcher; Neil and Glynnis are named after the Kinnocks, this Welsh couple who are in the European parliament now. Neil Kinnock was head of Labour for years. Politics must be important to Dad, or why would he do that?

Glynnis said, 'Artie, are you daydreaming again?'

And I said, 'No, I'm just thinking.'

She looked at me and said, 'You look like Mum when she's worrying.'

That wasn't good. I rubbed my face and said, 'It's nothing.'

I drew a map on the train and went over and over the directions with the twins. It wasn't a long walk and I was sure they could do it. Glynnis took charge of the map because Neil always lost everything. He was going to school with odd socks on and no English workbook that day, and Glynnis and I were really grateful it wasn't any worse.

They fell asleep when we got past Stevenage. Mum and Dad were in meetings in London, but Mum would be up in time to get us from Grandad's for bath and bedtime. I was sleepy too, but somebody had to stay awake or we could end up in Edinburgh. So I looked out the window and watched England speeding by. Neil fell against my shoulder and I put my arm around him.

*

One thing about the fog and the train journey, I had plenty of time to do my prep. I thought I was going to have a really good day at school for a change. But I was wrong.

The first trouble came when I'd barely walked in the door. Zack Taylor and Dennis Moore asked, 'Where've you been this weekend, Artie?'

And I started to tell them, but then they said, 'Was it Brazil?' And then they sang, 'They've Got an Awful Lot of Coffee in Brazil,' just like Grandad had at our match, and laughed really loud about it. I just kind of smiled and kept going. But I think even then I knew they weren't going to get tired of that one in a hurry.

With one thing and another, I was dying to talk to Matt in history. We only had one more week on the castle and had to do our report on Friday. We'd almost finished the building and just had two more ceilings and the painting to do. I came in and sat down in my place next to him, and tried to catch his eye to let him know

I had a lot to tell him, but he was interested in something across the room. It wasn't until we were actually at the building table that I had a chance to say, 'I think Zack Taylor is going to cause me a bit of bother.'

It seemed like, out of all the things I had to talk to him about, the one I should start with. Maybe if I'd started with something else it would have been better. But maybe nothing would have been better.

Matt looked at me then, and his face looked rigid, like a real stone. He said, 'Not that I'm speaking to you, Artie, but you might want to think a bit about how you use folk. Six weeks ago, you were going home with Zack Taylor and you even went to his birthday party. Now you haven't got time of day for him.'

He said this in a very low controlled voice, which was shaking with anger. And suddenly I remembered the football video and how I'd been so spaced out I hadn't seen Matt open by the goal. I tried to tell him it hadn't been on purpose but he just kept talking.

He said, 'Take me, for instance. I mean, I'm not as important as that Zack Taylor or owt, but for example, take lowly Matt Crawford. Thursday, we're best mates again. Friday, you don't bother to walk home with me or even tell me that you're not going to walk home with me, and I stand looking like a right prat waiting at t' gates for you when you've already scarpered. Saturday, I try to speak with you in t' changing room at t' Colliery Ground and you ignore me. You also ignore me on t' pitch until Mr Craddock shouts your head off. After t' match, you're too busy to find me and by then, I'm just a bit tired of finding you, so I just go, see how you like it. I felt bad about that on Sunday and came round to yours, but you were off *sailing*.'

He finally stopped for breath. I just couldn't believe it. I said, 'Matt, mate, none of that was my fault. I'm sorry about the—'

But he held up his hand. 'Save it,' he said. 'I'm not interested any more. You need to get real, Artie Connor, if you mind what that is.'

Have you ever tried to put a roof on a tower

with papier-mâché blocks? It's very difficult to do with just two people. And it's nearly impossible when one of the two people won't speak to the other.

I'd phoned Grandad twice to tell him that the twins were coming home with me, but when we got to his house I was ready for him to have forgotten and be in a panic. He wasn't though. He was making spaghetti bolognaise for our tea, and seemed fine enough.

The twins went through while I put the kettle on. We could hear the telly come on and we both said, 'Get your homework done first,' and then smiled at each other.

It sounds like everything was fine, written down like that. But everything wasn't fine. Even our smiles weren't fine. You could feel the not-fineness in the air, just like the fog the day before.

Grandad said, 'I know what you're up to, Artie.'

And I said, 'I don't know what you mean.'

And he said, 'Aye, you do.'

We looked at each other again, and I looked at Grandad properly. His face was yellow again, and strained. He said, 'You don't trust me to meet the twins.'

'How can I?'

It was out before I thought about it. His eyes filled up. He said, 'I've been a bit distracted lately.'

His cardigan was buttoned wrong again and his hair was mad. He was wearing his reading glasses and they were steamed up from the pasta water. He looked like a complete loon. I thought to myself, *I just can't handle this. I just can't handle another big talk.* I said, 'I'm going to do my homework, unless you want any help.'

His eyes spilled over and I felt terrible. He wiped them with the dishcloth.

I just stood there in the doorway. I wanted to cuddle him but I also wanted to choke him. It was the end of something for me. Before Grandad cried that day, I felt more or less in control. But now I didn't feel that way any more. I felt like I was about to explode, like the top of my head was going to blow off or something.

So I spoke a little rougher than I meant to. I said, 'The twins will come home with me.'

I didn't wait to see how he took it. I went in and stared at some maths problems. As if I could see the book.

Neil said, 'Artie, you know those two big kids on the bikes?'

But Glynnis said, 'Leave it.'

He did. And I did. But I thought about it later.

6. Who's Sorry Now

I helped Grandad do the washing-up, and he kept singing this song, 'Who's sorry now, who's sorry now?' It talked about hearts aching and broken promises, and asked who was sad and crying. It was like little nails going into my heart. Because I knew it was me. I was the one who felt sorry – about him and about Matt. And I was the one who wanted to cry.

And I thought Grandad knew that. It was the first time I realised that no matter what Grandad wasn't in control of any more, he was in control of his songs.

'Where do you get all those songs, Grandad?'

I asked him. 'How do you know that one?'

He shrugged. 'My mum used to sing it – your great-grandnan. You would have liked her, Artie, she was always up and doing.'

'How old is it? And how old is that song about coffee in Brazil?'

He turned around from the sink and sucked his lip for a moment. His rubber gloves dripped on the lino, so he held them over the sink, but he didn't move the rest of his body, so he was kind of twisted. He said, 'Well, let's see. I'm seventy-five and she sang it when I was just a babe, so it must be from the 1920s. And The Coffee Song is from the forties, or maybe it was the early fifties – it was a hit for Sinatra.'

He smiled. He said, 'The Rat Pack, that's what they called themselves, all the great singers – Dean Martin, Frank Sinatra, Sammy Davis Junior. They had style, Artie. And it showed in their music.' He was waving his hands around, dripping in the washing-up water and spraying on to the work surface and even the curtains.

I said, 'Matt's grandad is only fifty-three.'

Grandad sighed. He said, 'Aye, well, our family tends to breed a bit later than Matt's family.' And then he said, 'Thank heavens,' under his breath.

'What do you mean?' I didn't understand.

He did that twisting thing again. 'I was thirty-five when we had your mum. And she didn't have you until she was twenty-seven. That's a bit late for around here.'

Now I knew what he meant. I wasn't stupid. I'd seen girls not much older than I am pushing prams.

I'd been drying the same plate for ages. I finally put it away. My back was turned when Grandad said, 'That's why I'm so old, Artie.'

I wanted to cry. I didn't know why, but I wanted to cry more than I'd wanted to cry for a long time. Grandad came and cuddled me around my back, just as I was standing there, and I kind of leaned into him. But I forgot about how big I was. He kind of staggered and I had to put my arm around him, too, to hold him steady. We stood like that for a second. And then we got on with the washing-up.

It was Dad who picked us up, and it was late, nearly time for the twins' bath. I finished my prep at the kitchen table while he got them down, and then it was nearly my turn. I was tired, too; I was ready for bed. But Dad came and sat down with me for a minute.

He said, 'I watched a bit of that video again. You need new boots.'

Yeah, I did. I kept forgetting to mention it. Mine were going at the heel and the toes, and they felt a bit tight. He asked, 'Got your eye on any?'

I shrugged. I said, 'The new Reeboks look pretty good.'

'They ought to be, the prices they charge.' We looked at each other. Dad can get anything from Nike or Puma free. But Reeboks we have to pay for. Still, we both knew the latest Reebok boot was the best for me and the way I play. We didn't have to say any of this. We just looked at each other and kind of understood each other.

Dad reached into his pocket and took out his money clip. He passed me two fifties and a twenty. He said, 'Make sure they're decent. Don't just buy them in the box.'

I said, 'Thanks, Dad,' because some dads wouldn't have, you know. Some dads would have said, 'Have the Nikes or the Pumas.'

Dad said, 'I sent a copy of the video to Mark.' He meant Mark Gothwaite, the Under Nineteens manager. I winced, thinking about the first half. Dad said, 'I told him to fast-forward.' And then he stood up and ruffled my hair.

I started to pack up my bag and I heard Dad going into the study. And then it was strange – I felt like all my bones had just been pulled out or something. I laid my head down on the table, right on my maths prep. Half my head was on my workbook and half was on my textbook, but it didn't feel uncomfortable. It didn't feel anything. *I* didn't feel anything. I felt numb.

It only lasted a second. Then I got my stuff together and went up to bed.

*

I slept in a T-shirt and boxers. It was starting to get cold and my windows were wide open. Oh, and I can't ever keep my arms inside my duvet. I don't know why. I woke up freezing and went to shut my windows. And my mum was sitting on the bottom of my bed.

I nearly jumped out of my skin.

She said, 'Oh, did I frighten you, sweetheart? I'm sorry.'

'What are you doing in here?' I asked.

'I come in here all the time,' she said, 'just to make sure you've got everything.'

'But you're just sitting there.'

'I do that, too. I take five minutes and just watch you sleep.'

I shivered a little. 'I think that might be described as sick, Mum,' I said.

She said, 'Get back into bed.'

There was just a little light from the street outside. I could barely see her face. She moved up a little and put her hand on my forehead. It was warm. She was always warmer than I was.

She said, 'It seems like yesterday you were

just a baby. And look at you now! Almost a young man. It goes so fast.'

I was sleepy and I closed my eyes. But what she said next made me open them again, made me open them *wide*.

'I'm pregnant, Artie.'

No! I thought. *Oh, no!* Grandad might *just* last until the twins could take care of themselves, but he'd never make it with a baby. *I'd* never make it with a baby. And Mum would take time off, like she always did. She'd notice how loony Grandad was and he'd end up in a hospital or something. It was a disaster.

'Aren't you happy, Artie? Don't you want another brother or sister?'

I couldn't say anything at all. I just closed my eyes and pretended to be asleep. I don't think Mum was fooled, but she didn't try to talk to me any more. After a few minutes, she left. And I lay awake for hours, staring at the ceiling and wondering what else could go wrong.

*

I found out at breakfast. Actually, a little before. Dad, under the impression I'd been asleep since nine thirty, decided to wake me up for a little ball-control work at five. At six o'clock, someone rang the doorbell.

The only people who ever ring our doorbell are the postman and the other delivery people, like FedEx and UPS. Usually bringing samples or contracts or things like that. My dad looked at me and rolled his eyes. He said, 'You get it, will you, Artie? I'm going to move the target.'

So I opened the door, and it was the police.

It's quite a shock when that happens. There was a lady officer and a man officer, all in dark uniforms that kind of screamed the word 'serious'. The lady spoke. 'Are your parents here? We need to speak to them.'

I invited them in and went to get my dad, but he'd seen them through the big lounge windows and was already coming.

The man officer kind of looked at me and then at Dad, and Dad said, 'Could you bring us some coffee, Artie? I just made a pot.'

So I had to go into the kitchen. It took me for ever to find the tray and everything, and then the milk was off and I had to open another carton. Mum has to store the sugar up high, out of Neil's reach, but I found that eventually, too.

And all the time I was thinking, 'Is it Grandad?' Because that's one thing the police do – they come and tell you if someone's died. And on telly they always send a lady to do it.

When I walked in, I could tell they'd just finished talking about something serious. There was that feeling in the air. I put the tray on the table and started to go. But then I didn't. I stayed. No one told me to go, so I stayed.

The police did their coffee the way they liked it. They'd already taken off their hats. They didn't look quite as serious with their hats off, but I still thought the way their dark uniforms looked on the cream sofa was impressive.

The man looked at me and smiled. He said, 'Hard to believe you're only twelve years old, Mr Connor. You're a big un all right.'

Usually, it makes me feel uncomfortable when people talk about my size. I get kind of clumsy. But he was smiling in a really friendly way, like he understood what it was like to be big and strong and twelve years old. And then he said, 'If you do well in school, we'll always have a place for you on the force.'

Something clicked inside me. I can't describe it properly. It was like a bit of a puzzle – the last bit, fitting into place. Or like having a drink of water when you're really thirsty. I didn't even really realise it then, I just knew it made me feel good, what he'd said. And I smiled back at him.

And then I remembered they must have come for a reason and I stopped.

I said, 'Is it Grandad? Is Grandad all right?'

And Dad said, 'It's not Grandad.' I hadn't really looked at Dad, but the way he spoke made me. He looked like I'd felt the night before – numb. He said, 'It's the twins. They think someone might be planning to kidnap the twins.'

7. These Foolish Things Remind Me of You

Dad sent me upstairs to shower and dress. When I came down, the officers had gone. We were standing by the toaster. I could hear Mum moving around upstairs. It was almost time to get the twins up. Dad said, 'They told me they didn't think it was a very serious threat. Not to bother with hiring security. They said security made more problems than it solved, half the time.'

He rubbed his face. 'I have to tell them to watch out,' he said. I looked up at him. He sighed. This morning, he'd looked quite happy and kind of... *well*. He'd looked not sick, if you see what I mean? Clean and rosy-faced and kind of normal. But that had all gone; he had that patchy yellow look again. He said, 'Maybe you've made too much money when you have to tell two eight-year-old kids that...' He sighed again.

He said, 'I rang Henry.' Henry is my grandad's name. The toast popped up and Dad took it out of the toaster and put some butter on it. He gave me one slice and took the other. I was starving. I'm usually starving. I bit right into it, even though I was wondering what Dad was going to say next.

I didn't have to wait long. He didn't take a bite. Instead he said, 'Do you ever think your grandad's getting a bit out of it?'

I took another bite quickly so I didn't have to answer. I just shrugged. Now, that doesn't sound like a lie, but it was. If I'd taken even a moment to think about it, I would have told Dad right then. I mean, there's important and then there's *important* if you see what I mean. I didn't want Grandad to get into any trouble, but the twins' safety was *important*. I realised that right after I'd shrugged. But I'd already done it and Dad had gone off on his own train of thought.

He said, 'Yeah, I think he's OK, too. He must have been a bit sleepy. He kept telling me not to forget to tell Tony, and then he said, Artie. Tell Artie. I said I *had* told you.' Dad got this far-away look for a moment, and then he reached into the pocket of his tracksuit bottoms and took out his phone. He said, 'Sorry, mate, I'd better take this one,' and disappeared into the study.

I was so angry at myself walking up the stairs that I think I would have thrown myself down the things if I didn't have so much to do. I'd blown it. It was like that David Batty penalty. I was too young to pay much attention to it at the time, but I'd seen it a zillion times on video. His moment. Gone.

It was only about seven o'clock, but Mum was already talking as well when I passed her bedroom. Glynnis was awake, reading, and Neil was asleep, really sound asleep; I had to jump on him a couple of times to get him to wake up. They both protested at the early wake-up, but both stopped when I told them Dad needed to talk to them about something important.

They could dress themselves. I just had to make sure Neil didn't fall asleep while he was putting on his socks. I just kind of hung around, waiting for them, packing up my stuff in my room and listening to Mum move around.

Mum and the baby.

And suddenly I was really glad about the baby, even though everything was so messed up. I couldn't imagine life without Neil and Glynnis. I mean, they're complete pains most of the time, but still, I really do care about them. Sometimes it surprises me just how much. And standing there, I realised I already cared about the baby that exact same way.

Mum stopped talking and I knocked on her door.

She called, 'Come in'. She was still in her nightie and she looked terrible, really pale. She waved her hand at me and told me to shut the door. She said, 'If the twins see me like this, they'll think I'm dying.'

'Have you been sick?' I asked, and then wished I hadn't because it made her gulp.

She nodded. 'Seven times, and still counting.' She sat down in the easy chair and closed her eyes. She said, 'I'm too old to do this.'

I saw the bottle of Sprite on the little table, so I didn't ask if she had it. She drank loads of it with the twins. It was the only way she could get through the mornings. I said, 'I just came to tell you that I *am* happy.'

Mum pulled me over and hugged me really hard. She said, 'I'm so glad, Artie. I so wanted you to be.' She put my hand on her tummy and said, 'You can't feel anything yet, but it can feel you.' And then she bent over a little and spoke to her stomach, saying, 'This is your big brother Artie.'

Dad walked in. He said to Mum, 'We've got something else to tell the twins this morning, I'm afraid.'

He nodded me out the door, so I didn't see how Mum took it. But her eyes were red when she came down in her pyjamas, so I don't think she took it too well.

*

The twins were quiet on the way to school. It was a lot for them to take in: the new baby; the thought they might be targeted for a kidnap. Dad had phoned the headmistress, so they'd be watched extra carefully at playtime.

When we got to the gates, Glynnis looked at me. She said, 'What are we going to do, Artie? We can't walk to your school on our own again, can we?'

But I'd been thinking. I said, 'I'll be here. I'll be here when you get out.'

Neil looked relieved and ran ahead to where a few of his mates were waiting outside the doors. But Glynnis looked at me again. She said, 'Your lessons don't finish until half an hour after ours. How are you going to manage it?'

I said, 'That's not your problem. You just watch yourself. That's your problem.' And then she seemed satisfied, too.

Which was great, but it was Tuesday. I had to get to Bon Vue to train after school. And I had no idea how I was going to get out of my last period.

'What did you do last night, Artie? Go to Brazil?' That was first period.

'What would you like to drink, Artie? Coffee?' That was at lunch.

'Where are you going, Artie? Brazil?' That was after lunch.

'Would you like a snack, Artie? I've got some Brazil nuts.' That was fourth period.

And each time, Zack and his growing number of helpers would sing, 'They've Got an Awful Lot of Coffee in Brazil.'

Now, I just ignored it. But it's rather hard to ignore it when there's twenty people singing it at you, like there was on the way to fourth period. And what made it worse was that I couldn't help thinking about what Matt said. It didn't make it right for them to torment me. And it didn't make it feel any better. But because of what Matt said, I couldn't help but understand why Zack and the others were so pissed off with me. I'd been an arse, no doubt about it, and kept *on* being an arse when I just suddenly stopped hanging around with them.

Having loads of people singing at you was embarrassing. But *thinking* that way is what made my face go red. I mean, I didn't deserve to be treated like that, nobody does. But at the same time, I could see *why* they wanted to get at me. *That* was what made me really ashamed of myself. *That* was what made it hurt.

Matt was always around when it happened. He didn't sing, but he seemed to be kind of glad that they were tormenting me. And that made it hurt even more.

Mr Jankovich just looked at me when I told him I had to go. He said, 'Sit down, Artie, you aren't going anywhere.'

I'd put all my things in my bag and everything. I didn't know what to do. I just stood there. I didn't sit down like he told me to, but I didn't walk out the door either.

Mr Jankovich didn't look as tired as he had the week before. He looked like he usually does – pretty young and up for anything. Including, I thought, making a bit of a scene over a pupil leaving his classroom.

I'd used the dentist this time, and the same, 'I handed my slip in weeks ago' thing. So, standing there, I said, 'It costs money if you don't turn up, Mr Jankovich.'

He said, 'No slip, no go, Artie.'

I said, 'Well, what can I do? I don't know what they did with it.'

Dennis Moore was in our maths class. He said, 'Maybe they sent it to Brazil,' and everyone laughed.

Mr Jankovich motioned me outside the door. He stood there with the chalk in his hand and looked me in the eye. I looked him back. He said, 'I could get into a lot of trouble if something happened to you when you were out of school without a signed slip.'

So now if something happened to me it would also mess up Mr Jankovich's life. He'd get the sack and I'd be taking food out of his wife and baby's mouths. It was horrible, but it didn't change anything. I said, 'I'm not lying, Mr Jankovich. I really have to go.'

He said, 'You'd better, Artie. I'm trusting you.'

I think that was the very worst moment, actually. The day after was bad, and the day after that the whole thing just... well, you'll see. But that moment was actually the very, very worst. Walking down the hall with his eyes on my back, knowing I was letting him down on purpose.

They were a bit funny at English Martyrs. They knew who I was – they'd been teaching me just a couple of years ago. But they were still funny about letting the twins go with me. We were in Sister Bernadette's office and she tried to ring my parents at home to make sure it was all right, but of course she couldn't get them; there's never anyone there.

So then she rang Grandad. She said, 'Mr Wentworth? I have your Artie here, wanting to pick up Neil and Glynnis. Do you think, under the circumstances, that's wise?'

I don't know what he said. She frowned. She gets this crease between her eyes when she frowns. Sister Bernadette is the headmistress at English Martyrs, and she would really be quite a nice-looking lady if she wore make-up and things like other ladies. But she's a nun, so she doesn't, and things like her frown crease really show. She has these eyes – they're a really special colour of blue, like turquoise. It always kind of surprises you that she's got these amazing eyes and is quite nice-looking.

She kind of bored into me with them. She looked worried. Her face had that kind of drawn-down look that my mum's gets when she's worried. It didn't get pinched like my mum's, though. She didn't have the same kind of cheeks.

'You're quite clear what I'm asking, Mr Wentworth?' she said. 'I'm asking if you want me to release Neil and Glynnis into *Artie's* care.'

She listened a bit more and then said, 'Very well, then,' and put the phone down.

She nodded. 'You may go.' The three of us exploded like a cannon out of her office and nearly ran out the door of the school.

'Whew!' Neil said. 'That was close.'

Glynnis looked up at me. She said, 'We can't do this every day. How did you get out of your last period?'

I told her not to worry about it.

But I was.

We walked along Dewsbury Road. I'd walked along it a thousand times, but I was looking around now, as though there was something there that was going to solve our problem.

And then I saw it. A taxi rank. Minicabs. I said, 'Wait a moment,' to the twins and then, 'Wait' again, while I thought. The reason I'd never noticed the taxi rank is because taking a taxi was always completely out of my budget. I know Mum and Dad have done really well, but I get terrible pocket money, easily the worst in my year – only a fiver a week. And Dad won't let me get a job because of training.

So even though I'd walked past the taxi rank a million times, I'd never seen it because for me it might as well not exist. But now I had a hundred and twenty quid in my kegs. And things looked a little different.

I said, 'Wait right here.' And I went into the office, just to see.

It was a really nasty place. Kind of a shed with

a bench around the sides and a glass window that was streaked. There was an overflowing ashtray in the corner that reeked and the guy in the office was smoking while he talked on the phone. He had the kind of body that made you think 'heart attack' when you saw him smoking, and his face was stubbly and kind of unwashed-looking, like he hadn't been to bed in days.

Then he looked up at me and his face kind of… it lit up from inside. He said something on the phone and put it down, and then he came up to the glass and said, 'Saw that goal on Saturday. It were a cracker. Where d'you learn that?'

He was the godfather of a kid from the other side. I told him about the video and Pelé, and he slapped his leg and said, '*Knew* I'd seen it somewhere before. Bloody marvellous!'

He came around the side of the window where there was a door. He slid back a few bolts and opened it. And then he shook my hand, like men do when they're getting to know each other. He said, 'Mike Bashforth.'

And I shook it and said, 'Artie Connor.'

He said, 'What can I do you for, Artie?'

I told him. He said, 'I'll do it meself.' It was a tenner a day. I could pay twelve days' worth, and by then I was sure I'd have thought of something else. I paid him thirty pounds for Wednesday, Thursday and Friday. And then I brought the twins in to see him.

'Only him,' I told them.

I ran them the rest of the way to Grandad's and then ran to Bon Vue and was only a few minutes late for training, though it might as well have been hours the way Mr Craddock shouted. He gave me extra laps.

And then, to top it off, I ran back to Grandad's. The whole time I was training, I kept thinking of the chip pan catching fire, or Grandad just wandering out of the house into traffic, or bad men coming to his house and him just letting them in and them carrying the twins away.

Mr Craddock kept shouting at me, and when he did, it kind of snapped me out of it. But then I'd be just waiting for the ball on penalty practice or a set piece or something and my mind would be off, having these horrible visions of Glynnis being pulled about by a masked man, someone smacking Neil in the face, Grandad lying helpless on the kitchen floor... blood...

I was breathless when I got to the door. But everything was fine. The kitchen was all clean, the twins had finished their homework and were watching *House Doctor* with Grandad, all cuddled up on the sofa. Grandad told me my dinner was in the microwave, and it was. I went to pour myself some squash and opened the kitchen cupboard door where the glasses live.

My mouth was dry before I opened it. It got much dryer before I closed it. I just couldn't seem to shut my jaw. You could have driven a golf ball between my lips.

There were things Sellotaped to the cupboard door. First of all, three photographs: me, Neil, and Glynnis. All with our names in big letters above them and a label that said, GRANDCHILDREN. Then there was a list of everything he did for us every night, with a biro mark through COLLECT TWINS FROM THE FRONT GATE OF ENGLISH MARTYRS PRIMARY SCHOOL (DEWSBURY ROAD). The rest was still there, even ENSURE HOUSE IS WARM – CHECK CENTRAL HEATING IS ON.

A chart was there with meals. Tonight was STEAK AND KIDNEY PIE, CARROTS, MASH. After every meal, it said, SEE BOOK. The glasses weren't on the bottom shelf any more. There was a photo album there and an alarm clock. The alarm clock was set for 2:30p.m.

I opened the photo album and every page had a meal on it, everything you needed to do to make the meal, in order: LAY TABLE, MAKE BARLEY WATER, WASH AND PEEL CARROTS.

I didn't feel hungry any more. I felt like I might be sick.

You see, I'd thought that Grandad was getting better. But he wasn't getting better. He was just getting more organised at getting worse. I shut my mouth and my tongue felt like a dry sponge. Did he even know who I was, without the picture?

*

Mum came in. She smiled at me and I smiled back. She looked very tired. I slid the photo album back into the cupboard and shut the door. Anybody would have if they'd seen the way she looked. I mean, you don't want to burden somebody that tired with something that big, do you? And it wasn't just Mum to think about any more; it was Mum and the baby, too.

She said, 'Haven't you eaten?'

I had to kind of suck my tongue to get it to work. I said, 'I'm not all that hungry.'

She felt my forehead and as usual, her hand felt warm and dry and nice. It smelled good, too, of the cream she used and the perfume she was wearing. She said, 'Come on, you two, nearly bedtime.'

She didn't even see Grandad. They just shouted hello and goodbye.

The sun was truly down and the air smelled cold. Mum put her arms around Glynnis and Neil. She was humming and then started to sing, '...These foolish things remind me of you.'

8. That's Life

We got into the house and she said, 'Wait a moment,' before they ran upstairs. She sat us all down at the kitchen table and said, 'Were you very careful today?'

Glynnis looked at me and I looked at Glynnis. Neil said, 'Yes,' straightaway. But he always does that if he thinks you're about to give him a chocolate or something. 'Have you been good?' they'll ask. 'Oh, yes,' he'll say, the marker still in his hand and the drawing on the wall.

Then Glynnis said, 'We were as careful as we could possibly be.'

I just nodded.

Mum said, 'Good. Be that careful again tomorrow.' She sighed. 'It's probably just silliness, you know, but it's best to take it seriously.' She took out a sheet of folded A4 from her jacket pocket. 'We're all going to learn self defence. This man is coming round on Monday afternoon.' She unfolded it and we saw a picture of a big, smiling bloke. 'We're to learn vigilance, security and the basic moves of avoidance and escape.' She read the last bit off the print-out.

'Your dad wanted to hire a whole team of bodyguards.'

The three of us groaned, thinking of the stick we'd get at school. But then I kind of started thinking about the whole 'Brazil' thing and imagined these huge blokes with earpieces in and guns bulging under their arms walking around my school, turning their faces towards whoever gave me grief. They'd have dark glasses on and everyone would... no. I let that dissolve. Thinking I'm really special and kind of *above* getting hassle at school wasn't good. It was thinking like that which got everybody hating me in the first place.

I said, 'I think the self-defence lessons sound better.'

Then Mum said, 'Well, I'm going to ring and see if he can come earlier because...' She got this big goofy smile. 'Our weekend plans have been cancelled. We get to stay at home!'

Glynnis smiled for the first time all day and Neil and I went nuts. Mum closed her eyes and smiled. She said, 'I'm going to live in tracksuit bottoms and I'm going to hide my phone in a drawer.'

I said, 'I'm going to watch DVDs and eat popcorn.'

Glynnis said, 'I'm going to sit in the garden in the sun and read my new library books.'

And Neil said, 'I'm going to play games and eat all the yoghurts and chocolate mousse in the fridge.'

And the rest of us said, 'Oh, no, you're not!'

I was still laughing when I went to bed an hour later. I felt all warm and happy. It seemed like all our problems could be solved. I didn't know how, but they would be, I could feel it.

And then my dad peeked around my door. He said, 'I saw the light on. Could I have a word?'

I just nodded and he sat down on the bed, where Mum evidently sits every night.

He said, 'Have you bought your boots yet?'

I shook my head. I don't think I trusted my voice to work properly.

Dad rubbed his hands together. 'I phoned Gary today.' Gary used to go to school with Dad. He'd owned a sports shop before the big multinationals came into town, undercut his prices and shut him down. Now he managed one of the shops that put him out of business. Dad said, 'He's working tomorrow afternoon. If you go in, he'll fit your boots properly.'

He looked at me and I tried to make my face happy. 'Great,' I said. 'Thanks for arranging that, Dad.'

He looked at me again, and I knew I hadn't been all that successful at making my face happy. He said, 'Don't worry about the twins. It's probably just nonsense.'

'Yeah,' I said. My voice sounded hollow and fake. I tried to think of something else to say. I said, 'It's great about the baby.'

'Oh, yeah,' Dad said. His voice sounded as

hollow and fake as mine had. He kissed my forehead, like he used to do when I was little, like he'd forgotten we don't do it any more. And then he said good night and put out the light as he shut the door.

I knew how busy he was and how worried he was, about the twins, the offer from Labour, and now it sounded like he was worried about the baby as well. And he'd taken the time to actually ring Gary and arrange for my boots. It was really nice of him.

I was almost asleep when I remembered that I didn't have enough money to pay for them.

We never have any cash lying about the house. If I'd been Matt, I could have just nicked what I needed from the biscuit tin in the third cupboard. Everyone put all their housekeeping money in there. Sometimes it built up a bit, if Susie had been doing lots of baking or something and had saved some money on the shopping. Then they'd go to the seaside for a day. Once she didn't buy ready meals for six months and they went to Spain for a week. It was May and I had to say at school that Matt was sick, even though everyone on the estate knew the truth. We were so pleased for them, Mum didn't mind me lying to the teachers at English Martyrs.

But we never have any money lying about. Dad used to put his spare change in a jar, but now that he was in London so much he used it up on beggars. And he and Mum are always having to use their cards to buy silly things like sandwiches and crisps and newspapers because they haven't managed to get to a cash point. So even if I could have brought myself to go through Mum's handbag, it wouldn't have been any use.

Funny, isn't it? Richest kid for miles and not a penny in the house.

Neil was extra hard to wake up the next morning. Dad took me aside and told me that he'd been up several times with nightmares – big men putting their hands over his mouth. You'd have thought Glynnis would have been the one the whole thing affected the worst, but she seemed to get her worrying done in the day. Neil had kind of smothered it during the day and it had come out at night.

We walked to their school and I reminded them about a million times about Mike and what he looked like.

I was actually early when I got to mine. Everyone was milling around outside the doors. 'Hey, Artie,' Zack Taylor called to me, 'You made good time this morning. 'Specially since you came all the way from *Brazil*.'

I'd say about fifty people sang it. 'They've Got an Awful Lot of Coffee in Brazil.' They all started to laugh and then they sang it again, and again. I took off my bag and put it at my feet and just folded my arms and stood there. I kind of looked around at everyone. I caught Matt's eye and he looked back at me very steadily, but I noticed he still wasn't singing. If he ever sang, that would be it, there would be no going back. But he didn't, which I saw as a good sign.

I didn't go red like I had the day before. I guess, by now, I'd figured out what an arse I'd been, and that this really was quite a bit my own fault. But that didn't come as a surprise any more, so there wasn't anything to get really red about. I noticed how ugly some of the girls looked when they were angry, especially two I'd kind of hung around with and then dropped.

Then the doors opened.

I walked up to Zack Taylor and said, 'Zack, can I have a word?'

And everyone went, 'Ooooh.' Because I'm so big and Zack's not very and they thought I was going to give him a good hiding.

But I really just wanted a word. I motioned off to the side of the doors, where the grass grew, and he took a deep breath and followed me. Dennis Moore was waiting by the door with an anxious look on his face. I said, 'It's all right, Dennis.' But he didn't leave.

Zack was shaking. I put my hand on his shoulder and he shrugged it off. I said, 'Look, I know why you're doing this, and I'm really sorry. I was a complete arse.'

Zack was blond and pale. Even when he had

a bit of a tan, it was a pale tan, kind of goldeny rather than brown. His eyes were a soft blue. It was almost impossible, once I'd really looked at him, for me to stay any kind of angry. So it wasn't hard for me to keep calm.

But it was for Zack. He said, 'You don't know *anything* about me, Artie.' And I could tell he was upset. He shoved my shoulder. He said, 'I hate you. I hate everything about you. You're so bloody useless. I'm going to make your life hell.'

He shoved my shoulder again, really hard, but it didn't do anything. I mean, I didn't stagger back or anything. He was fast on the pitch, but he was a bit on the weedy side.

And then he walked away. It hadn't gone very well, but I felt better because at least I'd tried.

I ran into Mr Jankovich in the hall on my way to assembly. He said, 'How's your mouth?'

And I said, 'What?' without thinking. And then remembered, *dentist!* But it was too late.

His face shut down on me. He looked so disappointed as he walked away, I wanted to run after him and tell him everything. But instead I went into assembly. I was a little late but when I sat down in the middle of a row, the boys on either side of me moved so as not to have to sit by me.

I just kind of looked at the stage. As if I didn't notice.

And then Matt was there. He sat down right by me. He didn't speak to me or anything, he was just there. And all that long morning, that was the thing that made me feel the worst. I don't know why.

After assembly, Matt handed me a note. It was two pages of single spaced A4. And then he walked away. He hadn't said a word and I didn't know what was on the paper. But it had made me feel better, him sitting there. It was strange. It had made me feel terrible but it had made me feel better, too. I can't really understand it when things like that happen.

But I didn't have much time to think about it. The bell was ringing.

I'd almost forgotten that we had to do our history presentation the next day. Matt's note was all about that, about how we could work it by doing it in two different sections. He was going to talk about why the Normans built castles in the first place and how they used them. And then I was going to talk about how we'd built our own castle and what we'd learned about Norman construction techniques by doing it. He'd even written a list of facts I needed to know. Down at the bottom in bold he'd said, 'Don't mess up, Artie, it's my mark.'

Matt had to keep getting good marks to keep on at our school. He's on a scholarship. I couldn't let him down. I looked down the list and realised that I already knew most of it and that all I'd have to do to prepare was look a couple of things up in my history book.

It was a training night. I'd rung Neil on his mobile and he'd told me that Mike had picked them up. That morning, I'd snuck into the study while Dad was having a shower and emailed Sister Bernadette from Dad's account. She was completely taken in by the email, and even told Glynnis she thought Dad hiring a taxi driver was a very good idea! She'd waited with them, and only let them go when Mike arrived and opened the back door. It had been a black limo. Mike had been really nice. Neil would have told me even more if I hadn't told him to shut up and start his homework.

Training was good, even though Zack was there. There was a bit of nonsense in the changing room, with him whispering things about me to the other lads, but on the pitch, it was fine. I got paired with Dennis Moore in a passing exercise and we worked together for about five minutes with no problems. Mr Craddock patted me on the back afterwards and told me, 'See what you can achieve if you concentrate?' But it didn't seem to me like I'd *achieved* anything. It was just a nice, ordinary training session.

I spent a long time in the shower. When I came out, the rest of the team were kind of just hanging about. It felt strange being naked and getting dressed while they were all dressed already. I felt really too big, too big even for my uniform. My shirt stuck to my back when I tried to put it on and one of the buttons came off. Somebody laughed.

'Where'd you get that shirt, Artie?' Zack asked. He put in a dramatic pause before saying *Brazil*. But I got there first.

I said, 'Not Asda, where your mum gets yours.'

And then he said, '*Brazil*?' because he'd already started to, but nobody really heard him because they were already laughing. He sang The Coffee Song, and Dennis kind of started to sing it with him, but nobody else did.

His face got even paler, with these high pink points on his cheeks. He said, 'I've just about had enough of you, Connor.'

I was putting on my shoes by then. I pulled on my blazer and stuffed my tie in the pocket. I grabbed my bags. Everyone was watching me, everyone was waiting to see if something was going to happen.

I said, 'Zack, you're going to have to excuse me. I've got to go look at some new boots.'

And then I left. I was so angry and kind of...

I don't know... embarrassed, I guess. I was shaking. But I think I looked cool and unconcerned. Because that kind of thing, it was really important to Zack, but he didn't have any idea of what was really important in life. I had to run and catch Gary so my Dad didn't get his feelings hurt. I had to get home and make sure Grandad hadn't left SWITCH OFF THE CHIP PAN out of his written instructions. I had to make sure no one had come by to kidnap the twins after tea when it was dark. I had to somehow hold everything together. And there was a baby on the way.

I really didn't have much *space* to worry about Zack Taylor.

The boots were perfect. They fit just right and kind of gleamed in a soft dark way. My feet kind of turn in when I run, and these were made to stop that happening. The studs were fantastic, placed just where I used them. I could have turned on a five-pence piece in them.

I told Gary I'd come in and buy them the next day. I told him I'd left my money at home by mistake.

9. Fly Me to the Moon

I ran home and checked on Grandad and the twins, and scoffed a plate of fish fingers, carrots, peas and chips, washed down with about a litre of squash. I stood at the sideboard to eat it; I had to get somewhere, sharpish.

What with one thing and another, I hadn't been to the Crawford's for a while. Susie, Matt's mum, kind of just stood there when I rang the bell. She didn't say, 'And what do *you* want?' but she didn't need to. I could tell Matt had been confiding in her by the way she folded her arms and didn't ask me in.

I said, 'Hello, Susie. Is Matt in?'

And she said, 'I'm not sure.' And then she *shut the door in my face* while she went to see.

Susie has always been like a second mum to me. Last summer, she trusted me to baby-sit John while she took Luke for his injections. John was only two months old at the time. But now she left me standing out in the dark. I could hear everyone inside. They've knocked their kitchen and living room together into a big open-plan family room. They've got these cool beanbags that live under a shelf in the living room, enough for all the kids and two left over. I used to sit on the green left-over one. Once, I was there and Adie Laithwaite was there too, and he started to sit in it, but Suzie said, 'Oh, that one's Artie's, use the blue one.' Now I realised I might never sit in the green beanbag again.

The door opened and Matt stood in the doorway. Our houses have a step up to the door, so we were nearly eye to eye. Matt asked, 'Did you not understand something about the presentation?'

I said, 'No.' And then I said, 'Thanks for doing that.'

And he said, 'It's my mark.'

And I said, 'I know. I won't let you down.'

He folded his arms and looked at me. He didn't say anything.

I wanted to say all kinds of things. I started to say, 'Somebody wants to kidnap the twins,' but I thought he'd think that I'd think that was cool and interesting, or something. I started to say, 'Grandad's really lost it,' but I thought he might insist on me telling Mum. I started to say, 'I'm supposed to have thirty quid I don't have any more,' but talking about money was difficult *before* all this happened. I opened my mouth and I closed it again, not just once but twice, three times.

Matt watched me, his face drawn in like an old apple. And then, very slowly, still looking at me, he shut the door.

I could feel the warmth of the kitchen, hear his little brothers playing in front of the telly. I'd been standing in a yellow square of light from their door. And then, bit by bit, it all went away and I was alone in the dark, looking at the door we'd helped Brian and Susie paint black.

I felt so tired all of a sudden that I sat down on the Crawford's step. The moon was bright and so were the stars. There were little wisps of clouds, but nothing that made you think about rain. The air was cold on my skin, my ears and the place on my chest where the button had come off.

And something made me think of balloons. I'd been really into them when I was a kid, and still, like at Pizza Hut the other day, always got one when they were going, if nobody was around to notice. I'd been helping Glynnis fasten her belt, and mine had slipped out of my hand. It was a blue one but it looked white when it got above the lights of the car park, sailing off to the moon.

And I thought about me like that, sailing up, weightless, just flying away from everything. And then I felt a tug on my arm and realised I had these little strings, and down on the ground I could see my family and Matt and Mr Jankovich and Gary the sports shop manager and Mr Craddock, and they were all holding the other ends of these strings so that I couldn't go anywhere.

And then I thought about the moon, not like you do when you're daydreaming, but how it really is – cold and no air and no food or water or anything. And I thought it was probably good that there were all these people holding on to me, so that I didn't float away.

I stood up and brushed off the seat of my trousers. My whole uniform looked a mess, I suddenly realised. I touched my hair and it felt like it was going in all directions, too. It was just as well they hadn't asked me in.

Just then, I heard someone laugh and then say something, and they all laughed inside the house.

It wasn't good enough, this. It wasn't right that my best mate had a face like a drawn-in apple while I was sat on his step. I knew now what I had to say, the right way to start.

So I looked down the street to make sure Grandad's still seemed peaceful, and then I knocked on the kitchen door again. Susie didn't say anything this time, but she smiled. When she went to get Matt, she left the door open a crack.

'Have you been out here this whole time?' was what he said.

I nodded.

He said, 'If you catch your death and can't play on Sunday, we're going to get murdered by Doncaster.'

I said, 'I'm OK. I'm not that cold.'

We looked at each other for a minute and then Matt said, 'Well? What do you want?'

And I said, 'I just wanted to say I'm really sorry, Matt. For all of it.'

He wasn't expecting it. I could see him start to smile but then stop himself. Still, his face didn't look so bad any more. He said, 'Well...'

And I said, 'Do you think we can be mates again?'

And he said, 'I'll think about it.'

And I said, 'Fair enough.'

And he said, 'See you tomorrow.'

He shut the door, but I was already walking back to Grandad's. At least I started to, but I could see my mum and the twins walking up the street. Neil was carrying my bags, nearly staggering from the weight. I thought it would be good for him to do a bit of sweating, so I slowed down. Grandad's house looked peaceful. The kitchen light was off.

So, things were looking good: I thought I might have put paid to the whole Brazil thing; Matt and I were on track to being friends again... I just had one more really big worry to deal with, which I did down at the kitchen table once the twins had gone off to bed. Mum still had her jacket on. I took it off for her and hung it on the back of one of the chairs. I put the kettle on, but she said, 'No. I'll just have a glass of water.' So I turned it off again.

And then I sat down. I said, 'Mum, you know Dad wants me to get these new boots...'

She nodded. I looked at her, wondering how much she knew. I said, 'Do you know how he wants me to pay for them?'

She said, 'Oh, for goodness sakes,' and pulled her case towards her. She was muttering as she found her wallet, something about 'bacon-brained eejit'. She gave me one of her credit cards and said, 'Have Gary ring my mobile for authorisation... or wait...' She went into the study and got some headed paper and wrote a quick note. She said, 'That ought to do it.'

I couldn't look at her. It was all too easy. I think, in a way, I'd been hoping to get caught then. I guess I'd almost said the wrong things to Matt that night because I needed someone to talk to so badly. And now I'd said all the right things to Mum, so I didn't have to talk about anything at all. I said, 'Thanks,' and got up to go.

She said, 'Kiss good night. Only fair seeing as I'm buying your boots.'

So I kissed her warm cheek. She smelled like mint and tea and fresh air. It was one of her perfumes, my favourite one. How do ladies do it? Her day was just as stressed-out and busy as mine, and I looked a mess and minged. She still smelled wonderful and looked... well... now that I'd looked at her properly, very tired.

I said, 'Get some rest, Mum.' And she nodded, looking at her phone. I couldn't stay any more, thinking about how hard she worked and the money and everything.

I opened the window upstairs and looked some more at the moon. And then I got into my boxers and T-shirt, thinking I'd never sleep.

The next morning I could hear Mum being sick from the hall. There's like a million miles of their bedroom and a little dressing room to even get to their bathroom door, but she was being so sick you could hear it across all of that.

I woke up Glynnis and Neil and went back into my room to shower. It was then I remembered how mucked-up my uniform had been. But there was a nice clean one on the hanger, trousers pressed, shirt ironed and with all the buttons. The tie was around the neck, not creased any more. The blazer didn't have any mud or anything on it and the creases were out of it, as well. Shined shoes were by the chair and underwear was on it. My PE kit was in a bag and smelled like lemons.

The Daily Dozen people didn't come overnight; Mum hadn't rested.

Susie Crawford was walking Mark to school, wheeling Luke and John. She said, 'I'll walk Glynnis and Neil.'

I said, 'I'll come along. It's OK. I'm early.'

I said hello to Mark and Luke. John was asleep.

We walked for a while. Finally Susie said, 'Artie. You can trust me to walk the twins to school. I'm not gonna let them go under a bus just because you and our Matt are having a bit of a row.'

So I told her about the kidnapping threat. She whistled through her teeth. 'Blood and sand!' she said. 'Whatever next? How's Karen taking it?'

I thought of Mum being sick. I said, 'I think she's a bit worried. We've got a self-defence consultant coming to train us.'

Susie laughed. She said, 'Now that's our Karen – always practical. I'd be in tatters if it were me. I'd never let them bairns out of my sight.' We walked a little and she looked at me out the side of her eyes. She said, 'Your mum and dad trust you, Artie. And I reckon, with you being so big...' She kind of trailed off but then said, 'Still.' I didn't know what she meant, but I didn't want to ask.

I said, 'The police don't think it's serious.'

We walked a little more. She said, 'Matt and I don't keep secrets, Artie.'

I didn't say anything. I just went red.

She said, 'The twins could always come to ours after school. Two more's no trouble, and Glynnis is such a little angel.'

Which showed how much *she* knew about Glynnis. I said, 'Grandad's all right.'

And she said, 'Oh, I'm sure he is. But just if he's busy, like.'

We were at the school gates. Neil and Glynnis ran inside with Mark without even saying goodbye. I looked at Susie and she looked at me. Her eyes said, 'If you don't tell your parents about your Grandad, I will.'

And mine said, 'Everything is absolutely under control.'

She said again, 'Just if he's busy or summat.'

I said, 'That's a kind offer. I'll let Mum know.'

She said, 'You do that.' Her eyes still said the same thing. Mine were saying, 'Help me.' I didn't want them to, but I knew they were. She gave me a little cuddle and pushed me in the direction of school.

So, I thought it was all going to work out all right without anybody doing much. I was going to slowly get Matt back on my side. Someone else was watching Grandad. I could buy my boots. The twins were safe at school.

That's the way I kept on thinking. I thought that there was a way through it all, that I was going to manage. That everything was going to be all right.

Then something else would happen and blow it to bits.

*

When I got to my school, everyone was scuttling around the halls to first period and no one had time to sing at me. So I got the everything-is-all-right feeling again. Then the something-else-blowing-it-to-bits thing happened.

My phone rang in my pocket. It was my dad.

We weren't supposed to take calls in the hall, but I did.

He said, 'I want to see you, alone, at our house, directly after school.'

I asked, 'Why?'

He said, 'Did you hear what I said to you?'

I said, 'Yeah, home alone after school. But wh—'

The phone went dead.

10. Don't Blame Me

What with one thing and another, I hadn't actually got round to looking up those few things in my history book that I needed for our presentation, so I kept opening it and scribbling things down whenever there was a kind of dull part in other classes. Matt saw me doing it in maths and rolled his eyes like he was disgusted. I kind of shrugged, like, well, I'm working on it. And he nearly smiled before he turned away.

But Mr Jankovich had seen me. He said, 'Mr Connor, I'm so very honoured to have the gift of your presence throughout the lesson. I wondered if you could also favour me with your attention?'

I didn't say anything, I just nodded. I closed the history book under the desk.

It was a lesson about credit-card balances and payments, and how some cards had such high interest rates that if you just made the minimum payments on them, you'd never keep up – you'd just get further and further into debt to the company that had issued them. I knew all about this already. When Mum and Dad first bought their business, I was about the same age as the twins. They put everything they had into it, and were still so skint that they had to take out every credit card they saw and run the balance up to the max. We all sat down one afternoon and figured out how long it would take us to pay them off if the company failed. It made Mum look very worried, but it only made Dad laugh.

That was back in our London flat. It had a yellow kitchen and I used to sit at the table. I don't think I liked London very much. We didn't have a garden, and to play we used to go to a park, just my mum and me. I didn't know any of the other kids, except one who was at my school. I guess I was a bit like Glynnis, not having many friends. Well, maybe I didn't really have many friends even now. I thought about Matt and then about Adie and Ian, Rob and Habib and Push – the other kids our age on the estate. I thought about how I hadn't seen Push since summer and how much I really liked him, the way he joked about and how well he could play basketball.

Push can jump really well, really casually, not having to run up to it or anything. He can just be standing there with the ball, and then he bends his knees a little and then suddenly he's soaring into the air, giving the ball a little flick of the wrist, and it goes up in an arc so high nobody can stop it, right for the middle of the net. I can feel the tarmac under my trainers, the little bits of rock that grind when I shift my feet, and I'm just staring... my mouth's hanging open... and the ball is coming down, down, absolutely perfectly. I mean, Push had just been standing there a moment ago and now it's whooshing through the net without touching the basket...

'So, Mr Connor, which of these cards would you pay off first if you won ten thousand pounds?'

Push disappeared and I was back in maths. Mr Jankovich looked angry. I mean, I'd lied to him earlier this week. Then I'd been reading history in his lesson. Then after he'd pulled me up about that I'd just kind of drifted off. I only had about a millisecond before he was going to explode.

I glanced at the board, where there were three names with a load of numbers and equations underneath them. Barclaycard, Citibank and Marks and Spencers were the names. I said, 'Marks and Spencers,' very quickly.

Mr Jankovich looked at me, his eyes kind of narrowed down. He said, 'That's the right answer, Artie. But why don't you tell us why?'

I said, 'Store-card interest rates are always crippling.' This was a direct quote from Dad.

Mr Jankovich looked at me again. He knew I hadn't been paying attention, and I *knew* he knew, and he *knew* I knew he knew. But he still had a long lesson to teach and didn't want to waste time on me.

He said, 'Yes, well, see me after class, anyway.'

And Matt rolled his eyes again.

'I'm going to have to speak to your parents, Artie. If you can't concentrate, perhaps you need some help.'

'Don't do that, Mr Jankovich.' It sounded like I was begging. 'I'll do better. They've got enough on their plates right now.'

What he said next really surprised me. He said, 'So?'

I kind of stood there with my mouth hanging open. So he repeated it, 'What does it matter if they *do* have a lot on their plates? One of the things they have on their plates is *you*, Artie. And although you might be sure you're going to be a professional football player, injuries are common in your sport and you might want to have something to fall back on. You won't have that without a good maths qualification.'

And then I remembered the policeman, the way his uniform had looked so dark on our sofa, the way he'd said, 'If you do well in school, we'll always have a place for you on the force.' Then just for a second, my mind slipped out of the classroom. I'm running along the street, just like I had the day I went to get the twins. My legs are big. I'm all grown up. And my whole body is wearing this very serious-looking navy blue...

Kids were filing in. One of them pushed past me and I came back. Mr Jankovich said, 'You aren't even listening to me now, Artie.' He put his hand through his hair and kind of grabbed it, staring at me. He said, 'I've got to call your parents. I don't know what else to do.'

But I said, 'Do you need good maths to get a job with the police?'

And he looked at me and said, 'The police?' And then he thought for a moment and said,

'Well, yes. They like good maths and English. You know, traditional qualifications. Science and history are good, too.'

And then he smiled and asked, 'Are you thinking about—'

The bell rang. He looked up and saw his next class sitting in their seats, waiting, and then looked at me and said, 'Run.'

I did. I made it to English in about a second and a half. I only got a sharp look from Mrs Grady. She didn't say anything.

While I was meant to be writing a poem in English, I finished getting my history presentation together. So, when Matt came up to me at lunch and asked if I was ready, I could say, 'Yes.'

He was just kind of standing there with his tray, and I was sitting at the end of this table all alone and there were about fifty chairs around me, and I wondered why he didn't sit down, and then I realised he was waiting for me to ask him to, but by then he was moving away.

So I had to say, 'Matt?' And he turned around. I motioned to a chair and raised my eyebrows and wiggled them.

And that made him laugh and he came and sat down.

We didn't say anything for a long while. We just ate. Finally I said, 'Have you seen anything of Push lately? How is he?'

And Matt said, 'He's grown about a foot. He's taller than you.'

And I said, 'I'll tell my dad.' We laughed, because Dad has this fantasy that he'll be able to sell Push to the NBA. I mean, Push isn't *that* good at basketball, but Dad thinks if he gets him the right coaching…

And then Matt said, 'His mum's working overtime just to keep him in shoes. All his sleeves and trousers are too short. His blazer… well, the sleeves come up to his armpits. He looks a right mess.'

I said, 'I'm around this weekend. Maybe we could go and see him.'

Matt took a drink of milk that went on for

ever. I mean, I sat there and waited for him to answer for about fifty billion years, enough to make a new sun and solar system. Finally, finally, *finally* he finished and wiped his mouth with the back of his hand. He said, 'Aye. Maybe.'

And I had to be happy with that.

I was surprised how interesting Norman clothes could be. Neema and Sarah and Monty had made, like, a little play for their presentation, where one of them kept saying, 'Did you know?' and then telling the other two something, and then one of the other two would interrupt with 'Did you know?' and then the other one would do the same thing, so the facts kind of kept coming at you really quickly. I was surprised about sleeves. Sleeves used to be luxury items and you had to lace them to your jacket or dress, like you lace shoes shut. Only rich people had sleeves.

And then the boat was interesting, too, because they were pretending to be navigating and talking about the weather, and kind of worked it in that way.

And then it was our turn. Matt talked about pretty exciting things, like, suppose your neighbour decided he wanted your DVD player. How would you keep him out of your house? And people had ideas and he was sketching some of them on the board as they talked, and then he talked about the Norman ideas and how they were better than ours and better than the Saxon's had been before. By the time he was done, you knew quite a lot about why castles had been so important.

I hadn't really thought about *how* to say the information. I'd been too busy working on getting it. But I thought the question idea was a good one. I showed our model and gave a quick talk about how it was made and what the different materials were we used, and then invited people to ask me questions.

'What kind of stone did they use?' I managed to field all right.

But then it got tricky. 'Did they use slaves?' 'What was the mix in the mortar like?' 'Where did they get the cement?' It seemed like a sea of faces, and although I'd looked it all up and written it all out on a sheet of paper, I didn't know it by heart or anything, and I got behind on my answers. And then someone asked something I knew by heart so I answered that, and tried to go back to the others. Only, by then, I'd kind of forgotten what they asked.

It seemed to go on for ever, but finally Miss Kapoor called a halt. She thanked me very firmly and I went to sit down. Matt wouldn't look at me. His face was pale with two big pink patches, one under each eye. I knew he was furious.

He tore out of the room at the bell, but I caught him by his jacket in the hall and he spun round.

I said, 'Matt, I'm really—'

But he said, 'I don't want another lame excuse from you, Connor.'

He tried to get his jacket out of my hand, but I wouldn't let go. I said, 'Look, Matt, I hadn't thought about—'

He said, 'You hadn't thought? Oh, aye, that much is obvious. I don't know where your mind is these days.' Then he saw something behind me and he said, '*Brazil*?' really loudly.

I looked around and it was Zack Taylor, smirking at me. He sang, 'They've Got an Awful Lot of Coffee in Brazil,' and about ten or fifteen people sang it too.

I looked back to see if one of them was Matt, but it wasn't. He'd run off. I could just see his feet going up the stairs.

I went home straight after school. I got the number for the sports warehouse from directories, phoned Gary and asked if he could hold my boots for just one more day. He kind of laughed and said, 'There shouldn't be a problem with those.'

I wanted to ask him what he meant but he said he had to go.

11. You Lied to Me

It was strange not to go down to Grandad's. I didn't even have a key to ours, but when I tried the door it was unlocked. I kind of knocked lightly anyway as I went in, and closed it. I called, 'Dad?' but there was no answer. So I walked down into the kitchen.

My new boots were on the table, out of the box. That was the first thing I noticed. Dad had his sleeves rolled up. That was the second thing. And his face looked like it was a mask in that Japanese theatre, like he was the God of Anger or a dragon or something. I hadn't seen him that furious in a long, long time.

I started to back out of the room. It was an automatic thing, anybody would have done.

But he just pointed to a chair without saying a word and I kind of crawled into it. I felt like something was in my throat, but I couldn't swallow.

He let me sit there and sweat for a moment, and even in that state I could tell he was doing it on purpose. For some reason, knowing that made me feel a bit better. But only a bit.

'Your boots,' he said finally, and his voice shook just a little. I thought at first he was going to do an Alex Ferguson on me and throw them in my face, but he sat down and put his hands together.

He said, 'One hundred and twenty quid, Arthur.' He only calls me Arthur when he's either really happy or really upset with me. It was like getting slapped.

'Where is it?'

I still had ninety in my pocket, but I couldn't tell him, because I needed to pay Mike more for the next week. I started thinking about ten pounds a day and how – even if I tried to sell some things, like my watch, or this gold chain my mum had given me for my last birthday – that I couldn't keep the taxi thing going for very long at ten pounds a day, and that perhaps I might renegotiate the rate with Mike. And then I started planning what day I would do that, because the next night was Friday and Mum usually had something planned for Friday evenings, and Tuesday was training, so it would have to be Monday.

'Arthur Scargill Wilson Connor!' My Dad looked like he was going to burst. His face had gone all red. He shouted, 'Don't even start that stupid spacing-out trick with me because I'll have no trouble shaking you out of it. I swear I'd love to right now, don't try me.'

I said, 'Sorry, Dad.'

He said, 'Where's the money, Artie?'

And the best thing I thought I could say was, 'I lost it.'

I waited to see if he was going to hit me. He never had. Still, I thought right then he might. But he just kind of collapsed into a chair. 'You *lost* it?'

'I thought it was in my pocket,' I said. I kind of looked at the table for the next bit. I couldn't lie right into my dad's face. I said, 'But it wasn't there when I looked.'

'You *lost* a hundred and twenty pounds.'

I kept looking at the table. I shrugged. I said, 'I'm sorry.' And I sounded like I meant it, because I did mean it. I was sorry to have caused so much grief over what had been such a good thing – Dad buying me these particular boots when he could have got so many others for free. But there hadn't been any way round it. It was the only money I knew I could get.

I could hear Dad breathing hard. He said, 'You're to pay it back, Artie.'

I thought he meant out of my post-office account or something. I said, 'Sure. Do you need me to sign something?'

But it was the wrong thing to say. He got all red again, very fast, and went off to walk around in a circle. He was muttering to himself things like, '…my own fault, have it easier, ruining…' I didn't understand it all, but I got the general drift. He thought he'd failed as a parent.

Finally, he came back and leaned against the back of a chair. He said, 'You'll be spending your summer working in Gary's shop. I'll still send you to a couple of training camps all right, but you'll have to make up the time you don't work on the weeks you do.'

Almost everyone I know shops at the sports warehouse. I pictured myself in one of their uniforms, getting shoes for pretty girls, kneeling down at their feet and looking up at them, touching their legs.

'You'll be sweeping, cleaning and stocking shelves.' Dad seemed to really enjoy telling me that bit. 'And you can go round the car park and pick up rubbish and clean chewing gum off the floor.'

I shrugged. I'd still have the uniform. I didn't say anything and kept looking at the table.

Dad sat down. After a minute, I could hear him sigh. He said, 'Look at me, Artie.'

And I did. He seemed so, so tired that he looked ill. He rubbed his hand over his forehead and said, 'The way we live now, it might be hard for you to understand what one hundred and twenty pounds is worth to some people.' I thought about the Crawfords and nodded. I did feel horrible about the money, even though I'd kept it safe, really, and spent it on something important, really.

I said, 'It's OK, Dad. I know what you're getting at.'

He looked relieved. He said, 'You'll know even more after this summer.' He looked at his watch and said, 'I might as well get a little work done. I'll walk you down to your grandad's.'

We walked out of the house and his hand was on my shoulder, like he was steering me down the street, like I didn't know where I was going. But it felt nice. Dad has this really firm grip when he holds you. It feels like he's never going to let you go.

We walked into Grandad's, and there was no one about. The kitchen was in a bit of a state, like Grandad was just in the middle of making tea, even though it was a bit late for that. There was an egg cracked in the bottom of a bowl and some mince sitting out on the counter, going grey like it does if you don't cook it straightaway. There was some onion cut up fine on the chopping board. It all smelled a bit. Dad let go of my shoulder and frowned.

And then he saw the book, open to, THURSDAY. HAMBURGERS WITH CHIPS AND SALAD. He looked at the book, and I heard him breathe in hard. When he looked at me, he'd breathed in so hard, he'd sucked his lips right into his mouth, or at least that's the way it seemed.

He was looking at me as if to say, 'Did you know about this?'

And I knew all over my face was, 'Yes, I'm afraid I did.'

And then he said, 'We'd better find Henry.'

As we went through the living room, I noticed Neil and Glynnis weren't there. I mean, nothing looked like they had been there. No shoes in the corner, no books at the table, no bags on the sofa – nothing. Dad and I looked at each other again, and now our faces both said the same thing.

Fear.

12. Call Me Irresponsible

Grandad was at the bottom of the garden. Now, something you need to know is that Grandad used to garden a lot. I mean a *lot*. Our house has a wide but kind of short back garden, but the ones on Grandad's street go all the way down to the fields, long and narrow. I told you about the dahlias, but Grandad used to grow most of his and Nan's veg, as well.

Now he just had lawn and shrubs there, with a few flowers that came up every year. He did that so he had more time to spend on me and the twins.

But when my Dad and I walked up to him that

day, he was hopping on a big fork and digging up the bottom of the lawn. And then he kind of leaned over and looked through the dirt, as if he expected to find something. And then he dug up some more with the fork.

Dad and I looked at each other again. Dad said, 'Henry, where are they?'

Grandad looked up and blinked. He ignored Dad completely but he said to me, 'Oh, hello, Tony. I don't think Karen's back yet.' And then he started digging again.

I said, 'Where are they?' again for Dad, because Dad looked really upset, like he was going to shout or maybe even cry.

And Grandad said, 'That's what I'm trying to work out. There should be a row of onions here, and I haven't lifted them, that I do know. So I don't know what's happened. Nowt's been at them, they just disappeared into thin air.'

Dad looked at his watch. He said, 'Oh my God. They could be anywhere!' His hand shook so much when he pulled out his phone, he nearly dropped it.

Grandad was saying, 'No, I always sow them here,' as he dug into the turf again with his fork. I put my hand on his arm and said, 'Grandad, it's me, Artie.'

He kind of blinked at me. He said, 'I don't know where they are.'

And I knew he meant the twins, just like we did. Grandad started to cry. And then he grabbed the fork and started just... stabbing the lawn as hard as he could. We could hear Dad on his phone telling the police the twins were missing, and Grandad was just stabbing and stabbing and stabbing, and sobbing and sobbing and sobbing. And then he stopped and just stood there, his face so wet with sweat and tears he had to wipe it on the sleeve of his jumper.

Dad said, 'I've got to get back to ours. Someone may be trying to get hold of us.'

I think he meant for me to stay and look after Grandad. But I couldn't. I had to tell Dad about the whole taxi thing. So I ran after him. But I looked back just as I went through into the lounge, and saw Grandad sink down on to his knees at the bottom of the garden. I felt like my heart was being pulled out of me, right through my ribs and my shirt. It hurt *that* bad to keep on going, to leave him.

But I did.

Dad could still move fast when he had to. I didn't catch up with him until we reached the house. He was in the study, checking the faxes, his email, the answering phone. He told me to shut up when I tried to say...

Then he went to the house answering machine and checked that. There was a message, but it was from Matt for me. I never got it, Dad erased it, trying to see if there was anything else. There wasn't.

I said... but he told me to shut up and dialled the office on his mobile. He got put through to Trevor and told him the twins were missing and to monitor all communications, and I could tell, even from across our lounge, that the office had sprung into complete panic mode, just like my dad.

Then the police knocked on the door. It was the lady officer, with a different man. They sat my dad down on the sofa and stood talking to him. I couldn't really take in what they were saying and I don't know if Dad did either. His face was buried in his hands and he was crying.

I kind of tugged on the man's sleeve. I said, 'I know something that my dad—'

But then he kind of cocked his head and turned up his radio. He said, 'Go on.'

I couldn't understand a word of it, but he seemed to hear it OK. And the lady officer must have as well, because her face kind of changed. She kneeled down on the rug and pulled my dad's hands down from his face. She looked up at him and said, 'I'm afraid we've got some more news, Mr Connor. The sisters at English Martyrs have told us that the children were taken by a dark car, a limousine.'

My Dad screamed, like someone had physically hurt him. Tears were still leaking out of his eyes. He doubled over and held his stomach.

The lady officer said to the man officer, 'Go find some water.'

But I still had hold of his sleeve and I wouldn't let go.

It was strange, that moment. I felt like I could either stay in my body, or I could go off in my mind. I had this feeling like I was steering my body, like I was kind of choosing to be there. I held on to his sleeve, but like a puppet or something would, if it was clamped on. He pulled at my hand, but I clung on, my whole arm sort of wobbling as he pulled.

And then it was like I had made my decision and I was back, and I moved my hand until it was on his wrist and I said, '*Wait* and *listen* to me. I know something.'

Something about my voice made everyone stop what they were doing: the man officer stopped moving; the lady officer looked up from Dad; Dad looked up from where he'd been doubled over. I said, 'I know that limo. I hired that limo.'

*

I told them about Mike and the taxi rank. And while I was telling them, I was telling myself how stupid I'd been to trust Mike. I mean, here's this bloke I've never seen before and he's obviously a bit... you know, the stubble and the cigarettes and... When I'd finished, there was this long moment when they all sort of stared at me with their mouths open.

And then the man officer started talking into his radio about checking records, and someone going to the taxi ranks and Mike's house.

My dad jumped off the sofa and took me by the shoulders. 'How *could* you?' he shouted. 'How could you be so irresponsible?'

His fingers dug into my arms and my head snapped back and forth. It hurt a little, but not as badly as what he'd said. How could he call me irresponsible?

The lady officer made him sit down. And then she made me sit down.

She gave us both glasses of water that I suppose the man officer had gone and got.

She said, 'Now, very slowly and calmly, I want

Artie here to tell us all about why he was using the taxi.'

My dad spluttered something and nearly choked on his water, but the lady held up her hand. She said, 'Mr Connor, there'll be time enough for that later.'

I closed my eyes and tried to drift away, but I couldn't. I *so* couldn't that closing my eyes only lasted a second. It was just a blink, and then I was still in my body, still in the giant lounge. I said, 'My grandad's gone a bit loony and I didn't want to tell Mum because she's working so hard already, and anyway, Grandad's only got us and if we got taken away, what would he have?'

Which doesn't make much sense, as you can see. But she and the man officer nodded as if it did. And then she looked at the man officer and asked, 'Could you tell me your grandad's address, Artie?' And then the man officer disappeared when I did.

She said, 'Go on.'

And I said, 'So when Grandad forgot to pick up the twins, I taught them how to walk to my school to wait for me, but there were these idiots on trick bikes...' She motioned with her hand to stop me and got out her notebook.

She said, 'Can you tell me what their bikes looked like?'

'Can you tell me how tall they were?'

'Can you tell me the kinds of clothes they wore?'

'What their faces looked like?'

'Hair colour?'

'Eye colour?'

'Any marks?'

I told her everything, even about the spots. She kept nodding and writing and saying, 'That's really useful, Artie.' And then she talked into her radio a little more.

Dad had been sitting back with his fingers pressed into his eyes but he'd been listening to me, and at this point he sat up and looked at me. His eyes were red and bored into me like drills. I don't think I could have said anything else if the lady officer hadn't been right there, asking.

I told her about finding out about the kidnapping threat and about how hard it was to get out of my last period and about training, and then about the boot money and the taxi rank. She wrote down a few things and kept nodding.

She said, 'You know you should have talked to your parents about all this,' and I nodded. Dad had been crying and everything, but I'd been kind of all right up until that point. When she said that, though, it made me realise that if something happened to Glynnis and Neil it would be my fault. I would have caused it.

And my eyes filled up. I couldn't help it.

The constable put her arm around me and it was hard with muscle. Still, it felt good when she patted my back. She said to my dad, 'I hardly think you could call Artie irresponsible, Mr Connor. I'd say he's had a great deal too many responsibilities for a child his age. If he's made a mistake or two, he's done better than anyone could expect.'

And then my dad was there, and he held me so tight I thought he was going to break my ribs.

He stroked my hair and said my name over and over. He kept saying he was sorry and that he loved me and that he didn't deserve me.

And then I heard my mum say, 'What in the world is going on here?'

I looked up, and there was Mum. The twins were standing either side of her.

I don't remember a lot about what happened next, but I remember kind of scooting across the floor on my knees. Out of everyone, I chose Neil to hold. I grabbed him and kissed him (he had chocolate on his face) and held his round little body in my arms as if I was never going to let him go. All the while he was squirming and saying, 'Get off me, Artie! Get off, you poof.'

And I started blubbing again.

I was laughing and crying, and so was Dad. He was holding Glynnis in his arms like a baby and hugging her, and she was pulling where her uniform skirt had ridden up and showed her knickers, and asking if we'd all gone mad.

And then, while Dad was trying to explain to

Mum, I turned to look at the lady officer. She had tears in her eyes, too. And then she kind of gathered herself together and started talking on her radio again.

Mum said, '*Shut up!*' And everyone did, except for the lady officer, who smiled and turned away. Mum said, 'Everyone into the kitchen.'

We all followed her and sat down at the table. My boots were still there. She said, 'Now. First of all.' She turned to Neil. 'Why were you so late getting to Grandad's, and who gave you chocolate?'

Neil looked at me and his face asked, 'Shall I tell her?'

I nodded. He said, 'Mike, the taxi driver. He's so nice, Mum, he's really cool. He's talked to loads of celebrities in his cabs. He used to drive in London before he hurt his back. He knows the manager at the Alhambra theatre in Bradford and I asked him yesterday if we could go inside sometime and he said he'd try to arrange it and he *did*! And inside it's got...' Mum held up her hand and looked at Glynnis.

And Glynnis said, 'It *is* a very interesting building. And I *suppose* we should have rung to let someone know, but the only person we really *could* ring was Artie and we didn't want to disturb him.' And then she smiled very sweetly. Neil rolled his eyes at me and I rolled mine back; Glynnis's sweet smile really gets up both our noses.

Mum said, 'Why were you in a taxi in the first place?' She turned to my dad. 'I met them in the street. They were just standing there, all on their own. Anything could have happened to them.'

So Dad explained what had been going on.

The lady officer stuck her head round the door. She said, 'Can I have a word, Mrs Connor?'

But Mum said, 'No one is leaving this table until I get some more answers. Say what you have to say here.'

The lady officer smiled at her. She said, 'Yes, ma'am.' And then, 'I'm afraid your father is a bit confused and upset right now. We had some health-care staff come and they think he should go to hospital where they can have a proper look at him.'

Mum started to stand up, but Dad kind of pushed her back down on to her chair and stood up himself. But the lady officer shook her head, saying, 'They tell us that in most of these cases it's best if the patient goes by themselves. Otherwise they often feel the family has had something to do with putting them under observation.'

She wasn't smiling any more but her eyes were very kind. She said, straight to Mum, 'Honestly, ma'am, our best advice is to leave it until the morning and then go and visit him. He'll appreciate that more.' She gave the name of the hospital and said, 'My partner has locked up your father's house. Here are the keys.'

She put them on the table and we all looked at them. They still had the Morris Minor Club badge on them, even though Dad had locked Grandad's Minor in our garage two years ago.

She said, 'I know you'll have a lot to discuss. I'll see myself out.'

We all sat and stared at Grandad's keys. It seemed so sudden, even to me. One day he was there, using his charts and making tea and everything. And then the next day, someone was putting him in hospital for observation and we weren't supposed to go along.

Mum reached out and stroked the Morris Minor badge with her finger. She said, 'I can't believe it.'

Dad said, 'Yes, you can, Karen. So can I. We just didn't want to.'

Mum leaned her head back and closed her eyes. Two little tears spilled out of the corners and went into her hair. She nodded like that. She said, 'I know, Tony.'

Dad said, 'It wasn't fair, asking him to keep looking after the kids.'

Two bigger tears slid out. Mum said, 'I know. But he loved doing it.'

She pulled me on to her lap, as if I was still a little kid. She cuddled me and made me bend down so my head was on her shoulder. She said, 'This whole mess comes from trying to protect people from the truth. We have to learn from this. We need to start being totally honest with each other. No secrets from now on.'

I closed my eyes. It kind of hurt my neck to be bending down like that, but Mum was stroking my head and it felt good and she was warm as always.

And then Glynnis's little voice piped up as clear and cold as ice. She said, 'So does that mean you're going to tell Dad about the consortium that wants to buy the company?'

12. In the Wee Small Hours
of the Morning

You know when someone says, 'You could have heard a pin drop?'

My eyes flew open but my ears were open already. You could have heard less than that – you could have heard a mouse fart all the way in the garage. None of us were breathing.

Mum kind of stiffened underneath me. And then she said, in this terribly normal voice, 'Oh, that's nothing to talk about tonight. Look, it's even past Artie's bedtime.'

But nobody moved. Until I, very slowly, stood up from her lap.

I rubbed my neck. We were all looking at her.

She kind of squirmed in her chair. She said, 'I've had enough stress tonight. Coming home to find the police here and now Dad... I'm going to have to cancel five appointments tomorrow and he's going to be—'

'Relieved.' Dad cut in. 'Henry's going to be relieved. And you know it.'

Mum looked down and twisted her rings. She used to do that all the time and had to really work to stop it. Now she'd started it again.

She said, 'We'll put the kids to bed and then we'll—'

'No.'

I'm not sure I'd ever heard Dad say that word to Mum. We all looked at him and then looked back at her. She'd stopped twisting her rings.

Dad cleared his throat and said, 'What I mean is, I think we should all be in on this. It's a family business, and we're the family.'

He said, 'Glynnis and Neil, get this stuff off the table. Artie, put the kettle on; pot of tea called for. And stick some pizza in the oven. I'm famished.'

'Me, too,' Neil said, which made all of us smile.

I found seven pizzas in the freezer and put five of them in the big oven, but Dad had to help me light it. He also got a big tea tray together.

Then he went and sat down by Mum, who had tilted her head back and closed her eyes again. He said, 'I'm making an executive decision. We're all taking tomorrow off. No work. No school. So we can talk as late as we want.'

Mum said, 'I don't know, Tony. What do we have to talk about?'

And Dad said, 'We need to decide if we're going to sell or not.'

Mum's head snapped up, and she looked at Dad with her eyes all narrow and sharp. She said, 'You're not serious?'

He said, 'Oh, yes, I am. This is no way to live. This isn't why we worked so hard, for this – never being home, kids out of control, Henry pressured, you exhausted. We've got to start using our brains again. And now we've got five good ones to use.'

He disappeared into the study and came out again. He had a laptop on two long cords, five pads, a jar of pens and two calculators. It was like it used to be in the London flat when they were first getting started.

I thought the twins would get sleepy, but they were so excited they were wide awake. I guess the tea helped. And later, Dad got out the biscuit tin. Neil had two chocolate ones before anyone noticed.

It went on for ever.

Mum talked about how much they could get. Dad talked about how much we would need, looking at interest rates and projecting inflation. He wanted us to have enough to live on. He wanted to have enough to give the three of us and the baby a nest egg, to go to uni or start a business. He wanted us all to have deposits for houses, because he thought it was going to get tougher and tougher for first-time buyers. He wanted enough for a good nursing home for Grandad, if that's what he needed, and even enough for him or Mum to go to one if they lived that long and needed it, too.

At one point, Neil and Dad were working out projected investment returns when Mum said,

'But what will you *do* all day, Tony? I mean, I'll have the kids and the house to look after and the baby. But what will you have?'

Dad didn't even look up. He just said, 'Tell her, Artie.'

So I did. I told her about Labour and local government and the big oaks from small acorns.

Mum started to laugh, and she laughed so hard I thought she was going to be sick again. She got up and went over to my dad and pulled his head back so it rested on the back of his chair. She said into his upside-down face, 'Have I told you recently how much fun it is being your wife?'

And he said, 'I didn't know it had *been* that much fun recently.'

And then they kissed each other. After a moment I looked away.

We were nearly a million pounds short.

It was our fourth pot of tea, and all of us kept mentioning how nice the cloakroom toilet was. I don't think any of us had used it much before, but with all the tea it was getting quite a workout.

Neil and Glynnis were at last looking tired and fed up. Neil said, 'We *have* to be able to do it. It's what we all want. We *have* to find a way.' He looked as if he might cry. He kept going through the list of the things Dad said we needed to be happy and trying to cut them down or take them off the list. He said, 'What if I don't want to go to uni or start a business?'

Glynnis looked at the piece of paper with the total on it and used her calculator. 'It'd still leave us £800,099.50 short.'

'That's not where we should be looking,' Dad said. 'I know we've forgotten an asset. There must be something more somewhere.'

Mum shook her head. She'd taken out her contact lenses ages ago and had her glasses on. She was still wearing her designer jumper but she had on tracksuit bottoms with it, and they didn't match. I went and looked over her shoulder. She still smelled really good.

Down the asset list we went. London office. Stocks. Shares. Bonds. Our house. Our cars.

House.

House.

I said, 'Grandad's house! If Grandad has to go into a nursing home… what about *his* house? Didn't Dad buy Grandad's house for him?'

Dad looked at Mum and Mum looked at Dad. They stopped moving and doing things, they just looked at each other.

But Glynnis said, 'Don't be stupid, Artie. Grandad's house is only a three-bedroom semi. This is an OK area but it's really the wrong side of town. I mean, if *our* house was over by Sandal it'd be worth another £250,000, but as it is we'd never get more than £900,000 for it because of where it is.'

We were all staring at Glynnis – my eight-year-old little sister – and then we all looked at each other for a moment, and then went back to staring at her. She didn't notice, she was just talking away, saying, '…Now for Grandad's, we wouldn't get more than £150,000, £180,000 *maybe*, if we decorate and put in a new kitchen.'

She noticed us all looking at her and blushed. She shrugged her shoulders and said, 'There are so many telly programmes on about doing up houses. I think they're really interesting. I read the cards in estate agents whenever we walk downtown.'

It was all too much for Neil. He put his head down on his arms and started to cry. He said, 'I don't *want* to sell Grandad's house. I *love* Grandad's house.'

Mum and Dad looked at each other again, that same way. It was like they made something together with their eyes, a laser or something, like you'd burn your hand if you put it in between them.

And then Dad nodded and put his arm around Neil. He said, 'When I was growing up, I always wanted a house like this. A house like rich people had.'

We all looked around at the kitchen, at the big stainless-steel cooker and all the slate on the floor and the marble work surface and everything. Dad swallowed. He said, 'I love Henry's house, too. But I love *this* house because it's what I always dreamed of.'

Now Mum got up and cuddled Dad from

behind. So Dad was cuddling Neil and Mum was cuddling Dad. I put my arm around Glynnis, just so she wouldn't feel left out. I felt like there was something bad coming, from the look on my Dad's face. He started to say something, but he kind of gulped.

My Mum said, 'You can't reach out for something new, Tony, if your hands are full of what you already have.'

That's what The Old Man had said, that night on the yacht.

Dad nodded and swallowed. He said, 'How would you feel about going to live with your grandad? We could throw out a loft extension for a couple more bedrooms and maybe put a conservatory on the back.'

'You mean sell this house?' I just couldn't believe it. The house was so brilliant... it was... was... I looked around, remembering how surprised I'd been that there was food in the fridge, how I couldn't remember the pattern on our cutlery. And then I thought about how much the house was worth. Nearly a million pounds.

The difference between staying as we were, and being happy.

Glynnis was way ahead of me. She was already punching in some numbers. She said, 'How much is a conservatory?'

Dad grabbed the laptop and looked at some Internet sites. And then he told her.

'How much is a loft extension?'

A few minutes later, he told her that, too.

She rubbed her eyes and said, 'I think we're still £75,000 short.'

She leaned against Mum and closed her eyes. Mum did the sums again. 'She's right, Tony,' she said. Now Glynnis looked like *she* was going to cry.

Dad said, 'We need to work out what would happen if we take £75,000 out of the gilts, how much annual projected income we would lose.'

Neil rubbed his eyes and leaned over to watch Dad on the calculator. Dad said, 'Here, Neil, you do it.'

Neil had to be talked through the formula and he messed up twice and had to start again. The second time he swore. We all waited, even though all of us, including Glynnis, could have done it quicker. And Mum didn't tell him off for swearing.

Finally Neil said, 'We'll lose £2,780 a year.'

Mum looked at a sheet of paper and said, 'That means one holiday a year or no designer clothes. Maybe some years just one holiday, even with no designer clothes.'

Glynnis said, 'I don't care about designer clothes.'

Then for some reason everyone looked at me, as though it was me that wanted those things, as if it was all my decision.

Neil even said, 'Please, Artie.'

But Mum talking about holidays had made me remember my daydream. I said, 'Where did we go that one time? The twins were little and I fell asleep on the beach. You both kept laughing.'

Dad looked at Mum and then it was like they both remembered at the same time; they both started to smile at the same moment. Dad said, 'That was over at Robin Hood's Bay.'

I said, 'I'd like to go there again. Was it expensive?'

Mum smiled at me and said, 'We stayed in a caravan. It was dirt cheap.'

She said, 'Just a moment.' And she punched in some more numbers, checking the figures on that sheet. It had OUTGOINGS/LIFESTYLE written across the top. She said, 'We could probably afford one foreign holiday *and* one holiday like Robin Hood's Bay. If we were careful about clothes and eating out.'

Dad said, 'I think we can do it. I'll need to check the investment estimates with Barry and Graham. But I think we can do it.' And then he said, 'And it's not like we'll never be able to make any more money again. I'll probably do some consultancy work.'

Mum said, 'So we can do it. We can quit.'

And Dad started to nod. 'Yes. We can quit.'

Dad kept nodding, harder and harder and faster and faster. Mum was already smiling and so were Glynnis and Neil. They started to laugh.

I don't know what I was doing, but all of a sudden, I just crowed, kind of like a rooster. I was just so happy, so very, very happy all of a sudden that I couldn't hold it in any more. I shouted like that, crowing, no words or anything, just kind of a... well... a crow. I can't describe it any other way.

When I made that sound we all went mental. I don't know what got into us. We started jumping around the whole house and into the lounge, hopping on the leather sofas. Dad put some music on and we were dancing madly, jumping and dancing and hugging each other, and having fun.

We were selling our dream house and we wouldn't have as many nice things. Grandad was in hospital. I mean, if you think about it, we should have been gutted. But we celebrated until we were completely exhausted, and even when I went to sleep, still in my uniform just kind of rolled into the duvet, I couldn't stop grinning and kept waking up to laugh.

13. My Blue Heaven

I wasn't laughing the next day. Mum rang me from hospital and asked me to come. Susie Crawford was evidently in the house with John and Luke, looking after the twins. Dad was in a meeting on the M1. I was still in bed, so I hadn't known about any of it.

It was strange dressing in normal clothes on a school day. It seemed too quiet outdoors. And no one had laid my clothes out. I just had to try and remember what went with what.

Susie and the kids were watching telly, all huddled together on one sofa. The twins looked just like I felt. They were quiet and their eyes looked too big for their faces. It had all been a bit much, even though it had worked out all right in the end.

On the way to hospital I passed the taxi rank, so I got off the bus there. I opened the door and saw Mike inside. He was on the radio, talking to one of the drivers. I had to wait for a moment. He'd been smiling and laughing, but then he looked up and saw me.

The smile kind of dropped off his face, and he jumped up and hustled over to the window.

Before he could say anything, I said, 'I'm really sorry, Mike. I hope I didn't drop you in it.'

He had his mouth ready to say something, but he heard me say that and he stopped. He felt in his pocket and then went back to his desk and lit a cigarette. He didn't say anything, but he came back to the window.

I said, 'Was it bad?'

And he said, 'Coppers don't give best treatment to kidnappers.'

We looked at each other for a moment. I said, 'I should have warned you about Neil.'

'He's a persuasive little bugger.' Mike blew a cloud of smoke. 'Your sister's just as bad,' he said. 'She gives you this little smile and you'd do owt for her. Just the same with my daughter. She's nearly thirty now and still twists me round her little finger.'

I nodded and said, 'Sorry,' again.

And then I turned to go.

Mike said, 'You won't be needing us today, then?'

I turned back. I said, 'No. That's all finished.'

He said, 'Hold your horses.'

He took a ten-pound note out of the desk drawer and slid it under the glass. I said, 'I can't take that, after all we put you through.'

He said, 'Well, I took them to Bradford off my own bat, you shouldn't have to pay.'

Which is how I ended up going to hospital in a limo.

Grandad was sitting on the edge of his bed, his feet dangling above his slippers. When Mum turned round to see me, her face was pinched again. After last night, I didn't think it ever would be again, but it was.

Grandad saw me and said, 'Tony!'

I said, 'No, Grandad, Artie. I'm Artie.'

He held out his arms and I walked right into them. He held on to me, stroking my back. He smelled all hospitally, like the things they use to clean, even his hair. He felt kind of hot and sweaty.

It wasn't nice.

But it was, because it was Grandad.

After a long while, he let me go. He'd been crying again.

He said, 'Am I in here because I couldn't find them?'

Mum said, 'He keeps asking that.'

I said, 'No, Grandad. It was the twins' own fault. They were naughty, playing out late.'

'Naughty, eh?'

'Yes, they played you up. They were out late and didn't come home for tea.'

He nodded, thinking. He said, 'Yes, they can be naughty all right.'

I said, 'It wasn't your fault at all, Grandad.'

He sighed and rubbed his eyes with the backs of his hands. Then he lay down in bed. Mum said, 'He wouldn't listen to anyone else.'

I sat down on the edge of the bed, and Grandad put his hand on my knee. Mum said, 'The consultant is going to come round this morning. We've already seen one of his students.'

Grandad's hand fell off my knee and he snored, really loud. Mum and I both smiled. Then he rolled over on to his side, or tried to without much success, until Mum and I worked out how to lower the back of the bed. Then he got more comfortable. He didn't wake up through any of it.

Mum said, really softly, 'I'm glad about that. He didn't sleep much last night, the nurse said. And they didn't want to give him sleeping pills because he's due to be evaluated this morning.'

'Is he...?' I didn't know how to put it.

Mum kind of swallowed. She said, 'It's called Alzheimer's. It's a disease that kind of eats away at your memory. Your Grandad is really clever, Artie. He's been dealing with this on his own for quite a while. But he's so clever that he kept working out ways around it. He's a lot worse off than we suspected. They told me it's pretty advanced.'

She looked away and bit her lip. She said, 'The shock of everything happening has made him even more confused. I'm not even sure he knows who I am right now.'

And I said, 'He's always worse when he gets upset. When he gets upset, he thinks I'm Dad.' I thought for a moment. 'I guess anybody would be upset to come into hospital that way.'

She nodded, as if she couldn't speak.

I said, 'You know he didn't want to worry you. That's why he kept on going for so long.'

She said, 'Artie, stop taking care of me.'

I kind of blinked. I said, 'What?'

She hissed, 'Stop taking care of me, stop taking care of everyone else all the time. Think about yourself! Don't *you* feel *anything* about all this?'

I looked at her as if she was mad or something, and then I looked at Grandad on the bed and how small he seemed, just a little heap of a person, so frail-looking you'd think the wind could blow him away. And then I thought, *the wind* will *blow him away. He's going to die someday*.

Mum put her arm around me, tight, and I leaned into her warmth.

14. Please Don't Tell Me How the Story Ends

There's not a lot left to say. When the consultant came round, he was amazed how Grandad had coped for so long. He kept telling Grandad he was a 'heck of a fellow'. They had drugs they could give him that might help a bit, he said. Grandad really liked him.

Grandad had to decide what to do. He could have stayed in the house with us to help him, for a while, anyway. Or he could go straight into nursing care. One of the things the consultant said was that if Grandad was thinking about going into nursing care, it might be best for him to go while he could still adjust – later on it was going to be difficult for him to deal with new things, like where the toilet was and mealtimes and things like that.

Mum and Grandad kept asking me what I thought, but I kept asking Grandad. It took him a long while before he answered me.

When he did, he spoke very softly. He said that he'd been lonely since Nan had died and that he was very tired. He said he loved us all very much, but what he wanted most was a little bit of rest, and company during the day. He said the house had become a millstone around his neck.

That made Mum cry. She said she was sorry and that she shouldn't have made him do all that work and left him alone every weekend. She said she would do better, be home a lot more.

Grandad patted her arm. He said she was very nice.

The way he said it, you could tell that he was wondering what she thought it had to do with her, wondering just who Mum was. And that made Mum cry even more.

*

It was awful going back to Grandad's without him being there. He was still alive, but in a way, without his house, he wasn't. But also, in a way, he was always going to be there. I can't explain it properly.

We found notes and directions Grandad had left himself all over the place. He had little coping strategies to get through everything. He'd also hired all these people to come round and do cleaning and mow the lawn and all the things we thought he'd been managing himself. Grandad had been more than just a bit loony in one way, but in another way he'd been a total genius, hiding it as well as he had.

At first Dad couldn't understand how Grandad had been able to afford the help. But once he'd got power of attorney and taken over Grandad's bank accounts, he said he could, and not to expect anything in the way of inheritance from Grandad.

I was Grandad's main contact point. It's not usually someone so young, but for some reason

I was the one Grandad always remembered, even if he did call me Tony half the time. Mum said she would help, and Dad thought I could handle it, so Grandad's team let me do it. That means I was there through a lot of the transition to care. I had weeks off training and I missed some lessons and two matches. Sometimes Grandad got very angry about it all and shouted. Sometimes he cried. But most of the time he was all right.

It's a nice place, well decorated and everything, and the nurses are really cheery and upbeat. They play music all day long, things from the thirties and forties and some later things for 'youngsters' like Grandad who got the disease early. There's two other men Grandad's age he kind of hangs out with. I call them The Rat Pack. It makes them smile.

Grandad's got this patch of earth he can garden, and this young guy with dreadlocks called Blick who helps him remember when to water and do other things. Mum and Dad got me an account with Mike, so I can go out twice a week to see Grandad. Sometimes the twins or Mum or Dad come along, and we usually take him out at the weekend, just to the park or the cinema or something like that.

We don't take him back home. It would confuse him too much, what with all of our furniture being there, and the new kitchen and everything.

Our house sold almost as quickly as the company.

Everyone around here seems to think we went broke. People have been quite nice in a kind of horrible way; I think they feel sorry for us. Even at school, they've stopped the singing, and Zack doesn't seem to hate me the same way any more. Mum asked him to my birthday party and he actually came and gave me a nice present and everything. I don't see him as much now that I play for the Under Fourteens.

All the changes helped a bit with me and Matt, even though it was still hard going for a while.

I'm just so busy, with getting behind in my prep at school and now training with the Under Fourteens.

Then, one morning as I was coming out of the house for my training run, just after six o'clock, Matt was there, using our garden wall for stretching. He had some half decent Nikes on his feet, too.

We didn't say anything, we just ran together. When we got back he patted me on the back, and then he went into his house and I didn't see him again until history.

But he was there the next day.

After all those years of running on my own, I can't tell you how nice it was to have somebody to train with. We started to say the odd word and then, after a few days, we were talking again.

Then I started going over to Matt's at the weekend for help studying. You know, just a year or so ago, we used to be about even at school and on the pitch. But now, I'm miles better at football and he's way ahead of me in our work.

He gets things first time that I really have to struggle through. He's a good coach, though. He'll go over and over something until you think he'd be going mad.

I asked him about our falling out but all he said was last year taught him a lot about being patient.

Sometimes we go over to our place for tea and sometimes we stay at his. Sometimes we go find the other lads and sometimes we don't. It can still be a bit awkward. I mean, I have to ask, 'Would you like to come to ours for tea?' and he kind of *thinks* about it before he answers. Sometimes he says no.

But Mum says special people are worth extra effort, and Dad says you should never lose touch with the friends of your youth. He says no one else ever comes close to what you had with them. I remember all this while I wait for Matt to decide whether or not he'll come across the street and eat with us.

I guess I'm learning a lot about being patient, too.

*

We had the builders in over Christmas, so we all went to this funny little holiday cottage on the moors. We took Grandad. There was a wood-fired cooker in the kitchen, and you had to keep it going or the central heating would go out and we'd all freeze to death. The television was only terrestrial and there were big hills in the way of some of the signals, so if the wind was blowing hard you couldn't get them very well. Dad ran me in and out for matches, but we missed lots of Premiership highlights and he wasn't happy about it. But then we started going on long walks every day and telly didn't seem to matter any more. We were there for nearly three weeks and when we came back the house was nearly finished.

Dad said it helped that he had to come back to town with me so much, because he could keep on top of the builders that way. But Mum said they were glad to get the work around the holidays because usually nobody wants anything doing around Christmas. Either way, they did a good job.

I've got one of the top bedrooms and Neil has the other. It's shaped a little funny, but you can see a long way from the windows. We share a shower room and Neil's always complaining I'm not tidy enough.

Mum's getting quite big now, and she and Dad say the baby looks great on the scans. If it's a girl Dad wants to name it Maureen after Mo Mowlan. If it's a boy, he wants to name it Kenneth after Ken Livingstone. He's given all these interviews about getting out of the business where he says he got in it to help the sporting working men and women get a fair deal from the directors. It's so obvious that he's getting ready for the local elections. I'm surprised nobody's rumbled it yet.

We hardly ever see the people who bought our house. They came round and we gave them dinner and then they had us back to theirs, which was strange. But they always seem to be away. I hardly ever see lights on or anything. I suppose it's just like we used to be.

We were home one afternoon and the lady police officer stopped by with the man officer who was with her the first time we met her. Her name is Sergeant Southwell. His is Constable Coolidge. They came by for two reasons: first of all, they wanted Mum and Dad to know they were certain now that the kidnapping threat had been a hoax; then, they wanted me to know that because of the information I gave, they spoke to the idiots on trick bikes and found they were dealing drugs to kids at the school gates. The idiots got scared and helped the police find out who was in charge of importing the drugs.

Now the idiots are off in some protection programme getting help with their own addictions. One of the importers left the country but the other one comes to trial in a month. The DCs were putting me forward for an award.

Dad says the nomination will look good on my CV.

I finally told him about wanting to go into the police. I thought he might be angry about it, but he thinks I'm being very sensible. One thing he always says is that a professional athlete never knows when their career will end. You can just be going for an ordinary training session and all of a sudden – bang! – you'll get an injury and that'll be it. He used to use that a lot to argue for players to get more money. Now he used it to tell me that he wasn't angry, that he thought I was doing the right thing to think about *another* kind of life where I could be happy, as well.

He even found out all this information about being a special constable so that if I wanted to, and my club didn't mind too much, I could maybe do both for a while. And he's looked into the police pay structure and pension plan, and thinks it's not that bad.

I'm really enjoying it with the Under Fourteens and my dad's been giving me extra coaching himself. I've been staying in *the zone* longer when I'm on the pitch and I think I'm starting to understand what Mr Craddock means by a good training session. Some quite difficult things, things that I usually have to think about, I've been doing over and over until I don't have to think about them any more. In matches, they get just like knowing where the goal is or any other thing I do automatically. I think that's what good training does, it makes the list of automatic things longer.

Nobody knows if I'll be good enough to make the Premiership, but everyone Dad talks to thinks I've got a chance.

I've looked at police pay, too. A few years of Premiership money would come in handy.

My marks this term are going to be a lot better than my marks last term, especially in maths. Matt's coaching helps, and I've been working hard for a change. I've even done a couple of extra projects, like this that I'm writing for English.

And my mind is just working better. I don't seem to drift off as much as I used to. I don't know why it's easier to concentrate. It's like the daydreams just don't come to me any more.

When I walk through the door after school,

everyone's in one place, safe. Mum or Dad will be making tea, depending on how Mum feels. The twins will be sat at the table, doing their homework. If Dad's not making tea, he might be sitting with them, working on something of his own on his laptop, or talking on the phone. But if he is, Mum will be laid down on the big sofa, reading or knitting.

The lights will all be on. Sometimes someone will say something.

Across town, Grandad will be relaxing, eating his own tea, not having to mess with chip pans or kettles, maybe humming along to songs or talking to the other Rat Packers.

If I haven't been training, I'll sit down and start my prep, trying to get enough done so that I can take five minutes after tea and go see if Push or Adie or Ian or Habib or Rob or Matt are hanging around. I might play a bit of basketball or watch Habib on his skateboard, or just have a chat. Rob got a girlfriend last week. We've been talking a lot about that.

And then when I come back, I'll do a bit more

work before bedtime. I might have one eye on whatever's on telly. Or Mum might show me some baby stuff. Or Dad might show me something he's working on. He's doing some consultancy work with a promotions company that uses sports people for product placement. He knows everyone, so it's easy for him.

Some nights, Dad will go out for an hour or so and knock on doors, talking to people about what they want from their local government. He's still got months to go before his name goes on the nomination list and he's already campaigning. He comes home all fired up and talks to Mum until she yawns.

Whether or not he's home, I go to bed fairly early. I have to remember to put my things in the laundry basket in the bathroom downstairs, because it's hard for Mum to get up here right now. And that means I have to make sure I've got my uniform and my kit and everything for the next day. Mum used to make me bring it down to show her, but now she trusts me.

One of my windows is slanted, so I can see

the sky. Neil and I both have them. I put my bed under mine, and didn't want a blind. I lie there and look up at the stars or the clouds before I fall asleep. It's especially nice if it's raining.

I know none of this is very exciting to read about. My life is all completely ordinary now. There's nothing particularly special about any of it.

Still, I think I know why I don't daydream so much any more.

I did what Matt said. I got real.

wipe out
mimi thebo

'It's a monster. A big, grey wave, white at the top. It curls over into a whacking big tube. Mum is paddling like anything... I just know she's going to take it on.'

Billy is dreaming of his mother, Kitten Brown, champion surfer. After her death, real life lacks the colour it once had. But, with the help of new friends, Billy takes action... and in doing so brightens the lives of all around him.

hit the road, jack
mimi thebo

'I should have forgotten about my dad. I should have stayed at home. I shouldn't have been there at all. I could feel my heart beating against my ribcage. My mouth went dry.'

After reading the letters, Jack is determined to find his father. He knows he shouldn't roam the streets at night, but how else can he find out the truth...